THE TEMPLAR DETECTIVE

A TEMPLAR DETECTIVE THRILLER

Also by J. Robert Kennedy

James Acton Thrillers

Special Agent Dylan Kane Thrillers

Templar Detective Thrillers

Kriminalinspektor Wolfgang Vogel Mysteries

The Colonel's Wife   *Sins of the Child*

Delta Force Unleashed Thrillers

Payback	*The Lazarus*	*Forgotten*
Infidels	*Moment*	*The Cuban*
	Kill Chain	*Incident*

Detective Shakespeare Mysteries

Depraved Difference   *Tick Tock*   *The Redeemer*

Zander Varga, Vampire Detective

The Turned

THE TEMPLAR DETECTIVE

A TEMPLAR DETECTIVE THRILLER

J. ROBERT KENNEDY

UnderMill PRESS

This is a work of fiction. Names, characters, places, and incidents are products of the author's imagination. Any resemblance to actual persons, living or dead, is entirely coincidental.

Copyright ©2017 J. Robert Kennedy

All rights reserved. No part of this publication may be reproduced, stored in or introduced into a retrieval system, or transmitted in any form, or by any means (electronic, mechanical, photocopying, recording or otherwise) without the prior written permission of the publisher.

ISBN: 9780991814220

First Edition

10 9 8 7 6 5 4 3 2 1

For Ken Arundel.

THE TEMPLAR DETECTIVE

A TEMPLAR DETECTIVE
THRILLER

THE
TEMPLAR
DETECTIVE

A TEMPLAR DETECTIVE
THRILLER

"Non nobis, Domine, non nobis, sed Nomini tuo da gloriam."

"Not unto us, O Lord, not unto us, but unto thy Name give glory."

Motto of the Knights Templar

"As for the things that you will receive from the spoils, you can confidently put them to your own use, and we prohibit that you be coerced against your will to give anyone a portion of these."

Papal Bull issued by Pope Innocent II, recognizing the Order of the Poor Knights of Christ and of the Temple of Solomon, and granting them Papal protection.
AD 1139

AUTHOR'S NOTE

The word "detective" is believed to have originated in the mid-nineteenth century, however, that doesn't mean the concept of someone who investigated crime originated less than two hundred years ago. Crime long predated this era, and those who investigated it as well.

The following historical thriller is intended to be an entertaining read for all, with the concept of a "Templar Detective" a fun play on a modern term. The dialog is intentionally written in such a way that today's audiences can relate, as opposed to how people might have spoken in Medieval France, where, of course, they conversed in French and not English, with therefore completely different manners of speaking, and of addressing one another. For consistency, English phrasing is always used, such as Mister instead of Monsieur. This does not mean they will be speaking to each other as rappers and gangsters, but will instead communicate in ways that imply comfort and familiarity, as we would today. If you are expecting, "Thou dost hath offended me, my good sir," then prepareth thyself for disappointment. If, however, you are looking for a fast-paced adventure, with plenty of action, mystery, and humor, then you've come to the right place.

Enjoy.

PREFACE

In AD 1119, nine knights, Godfrey de Saint-Omer, Payen de Montdidier, Archambaud de St. Agnan, Andre de Montbard, Geoffrey Bison, Hugues I, Rossal, and Gondamerled, led by Hugues de Payens, approached King Baldwin II of Jerusalem, seeking permission to establish an order dedicated to serving God and protecting the Holy Land and the pilgrims visiting it. Baldwin agreed, granting The Poor Fellow-Soldiers of Christ and of the Temple of Solomon, the Temple Mount as their headquarters. Perhaps this is the beginning of the curiosity surrounding these great men, who quickly grew to be one of the most substantial forces in Christianity, with properties and holdings across Christendom, extending from the Holy Land to most of the kingdoms of Europe, little of the continent escaping their influence.

For a time, they owned the entire island of Cyprus, and through their clever use of what some consider the world's first checks—letters of credit—and at the time, an unbreakable cypher, they became the first major bankers of the realm, controlling the safe transfer of vast amounts of wealth across great distances, the fees allowing them to purchase ever-increasing amounts of lands and businesses.

But with great power comes great jealousy, and when kings unanswerable to the law become one's customers, things will never end well for anyone but the king.

The Templars would eventually fall, betrayed and

arrested on Friday, October 13th, 1307, yet their legend and their deeds continue to fire the imagination to this day, and this story is about but one of these brave men, devoted to God, and asked to make an impossible choice.

To give up everything he knows, everything he has devoted his entire life to, or betray the only family he has left.

Crécy-la-Chapelle, Kingdom of France
AD 1297

"What use is a knight that gets too old to fight?"

It was said more to himself than the others, but Sir Marcus de Rancourt shouldn't have been surprised when his sergeant, Simon Chastain, leaped to his master's defense.

"Sir, you are not too old to fight! Why, it was only last night that you bested three men."

Marcus grunted. "That was a dispute in a tavern, and they were probably drunk."

"True, sir, but so were you!"

Marcus chuckled. "Which might be why I don't remember it."

Simon grinned. "I assure you, you were quite the sight."

Marcus glanced at Simon. "Then I wonder who Sir Raimond was speaking of when he said a Templar Knight was seen accosting three of the King's men, then passing out before he could draw his sword?"

Simon shrugged. "I've no idea. I'm new to these parts."

Marcus laughed, slapping Simon on the shoulder. "You lie like a Saracen!"

Simon grinned, joining in. No longer so young himself, he had served with Marcus for the better part of two decades. His loyalty was unquestioned, but his friendship was what Marcus valued most. Simon knew him better than any man could, and since Marcus had

4

no wife or children, the sergeant probably knew him better than anyone ever had or ever would.

Though he was no longer alone.

The new additions to his life had driven him to drink, something frowned upon in the Order. Wine to quench the thirst was permitted, but in excess, never. Yet he could be forgiven. He *should* be forgiven. It was a one-time occurrence, not to be repeated—not after what had happened.

Marcus became serious. "*Whomever* he spoke of, it shouldn't have happened. I sinned."

Simon lowered his voice, bowing his head slightly as he checked the horses' saddles. "No one could blame you, sir. You have been through so much."

Marcus grunted. "No more so than many others."

"That may be, but just because others have suffered as a collective, doesn't make it any less easy for an individual."

Marcus mounted his horse and regarded his sergeant. "When did you become so wise?"

"It must be the company I keep."

Marcus laughed, tossing his head back, immediately regretting it, his left shoulder roaring in agony. He gasped then cursed. "Will this pain ever cease haunting me?"

"Never, if you keep straining it. The wound needs time to heal."

Marcus frowned then glanced about the sleepy village outside Paris. "I think there will be plenty of time for it to heal in this godforsaken place."

Simon mounted his own steed and regarded the area. "It is rather bleak, isn't it?"

"It's definitely not Jerusalem."

"No, but what is? Can there be any place more holy, more spiritual, than where our Lord himself walked?"

Marcus stared at the steeple of the humble church, then closed his eyes, picturing the land that had been his home for most of his adult life. He was a Templar, dedicated to protecting the Holy Land from the infidel Muslims, and sworn to provide safe passage to pilgrims on their way to visit the birthplace of their religion.

It was an honorable life, one he had no regrets in having committed himself to, none except one.

One he had never been able to reconcile.

A little boy burst from a doorway not fifty paces away, his face stained with tears, his cheeks pale beyond compare, almost as white as his wide eyes.

And covered in blood.

He sprinted toward them then stopped, his jaw dropping at the imposing figure of Marcus on horseback, in full regalia, his white surcoat with red cross impressive, despite the humble cloth from which it was made.

"What is it, boy? Are you all right?"

The child's eyes fixated on the cross emblazoned on Marcus' surcoat, then they rolled into the back of his head as he collapsed to the ground.

Outside La Roche-Guillaume, Antioch
The Holy Land
Four months earlier

Sir Marcus tumbled off his horse as the beast cried out in pain, a Saracen spear having pierced its front quarter armor. He rolled then leaped to his feet, swinging his sword in a wide arc as he cleaved the arm off the man who had thrown the spear, ensuring he'd never do so again.

He heard the grunt of someone behind him and ducked, spinning clockwise, his arm and sword extended, slicing open the belly of another of the godless infidels determined to destroy the Christian way of life he held so dear.

"Sir!"

He glanced over his shoulder to see his sergeant galloping toward him. Simon leaped from the mount and Marcus swung on, a Templar Knight most effective when atop a horse. He charged forward, into the thick of the melee, swinging and thrusting his way through the pressing flesh, his well-trained horse calmly following his commands, delivered mostly through the movement of muscles in his legs and feet, leaving his hands free for battle.

They were a unit, a centaur of legend, half man, half beast, operating as one.

And there was no more powerful force.

As he continued to press forward with his brothers in arms, the foot soldiers behind them cleaned up the mess they left behind, killing the stragglers, and finishing off the wounded, no Saracen left alive for long, after the wall of Templars passed them.

Today was a good day, a day that would end in victory, a day that would result in story and song, and they would praise their Lord for His granting of triumph over these heathens, then pray for the souls of those lost.

And despite the Saracens being his sworn enemies, he would even say a prayer for their misguided souls, for he was not one to relish in the death of any man, enemy or not. If the Saracens simply lived with their Christian neighbors in peace, then none of this would be necessary, yet they wouldn't. How much was their leaders' fault, he wasn't certain, but it didn't matter.

They were on the field of battle.

Which made their lives forfeit.

He swung again, his sword slicing upward, splitting his foe's face in two, starting at the chin, the body collapsing to the ground and forgotten as his next victim became his focus.

"They're retreating!"

Marcus swung again, and again reduced the enemy by one, before taking a moment to scan the battlefield, the enemy turning. He thrust at someone not privy to what his brethren were doing, burying his blade several inches into the man's chest before extending a boot and kicking the corpse off his sword.

And then it was over.

Cheers erupted from the victorious Templars and the other Christian soldiers surrounding them, the thunderous joy deafening. He turned back to spot his sergeant grinning, face and armor covered in blood, his own sword stained and raised.

"Shields!"

He spun in his saddle then gasped as thousands of arrows arced toward them. It hadn't been a victory after all.

It had been a trap.

He raised his shield, drawing inward as he leaned over his horse's neck, lowering the shield over his head. The distinctive sound of the arrows as they sped toward them was overwhelming, the battlefield now otherwise silent as the premature celebration was forgotten.

And then they hit.

Thousands of arrows slammed into the ground and shields, with some making their way through. Horses whinnied in agony, and soldiers cried out in pain as too many found their mark. Several impacted his own shield, at least two piercing the protective covering, though nothing more.

He closed his eyes and said a silent prayer.

The thuds of the arrows finally eased, then stopped, and he shifted his shield to the side to peer around.

Something slammed into his shoulder and he gasped, falling backward in his saddle, his horse whinnying in fright. He grabbed for the source of the stabbing pain, his eyes wincing and filled with tears, unable to see what had hit him.

But his hands found the source.

An arrow.

Probably the last one to be shot.

His beast shifted, then rose up on its hind legs, kicking out in fear and tossing him from the saddle and onto the unforgiving landscape, his head slamming into something, what, he did not know.

All he could hear were the sounds of the knights on either side of him trying to calm his horse, and the shouts of his sergeant as he neared.

Then a rush of silence as he lost consciousness.

Templar Fortress
La Roche-Guillaume, Antioch

Sir Marcus slowly awoke, his head pounding, his mouth dry as if he had gone without for days. He slowly opened his equally dry eyes, forcing himself to blink several times before he recognized where he was. And breathed a sigh of relief. He was in the hospital, a familiar place, though this was the first time he was a patient. He had visited many a wounded brother here over the years, and had been fortunate to have never been wounded beyond anything his squire could attend to personally.

He reached for his shoulder and winced, the very motion agonizing.

"Sir, you're awake!"

There was a little too much surprise in his sergeant's voice to not be concerned. "You expected otherwise?"

Simon appeared in his field of vision with a cup, pressing it against Marcus' lips. "Drink."

Marcus felt the cool liquid and opened his mouth, drinking greedily as his thirst was quenched, if only slightly. The cup was soon emptied. "More."

Simon nodded, returning a moment later, the task repeated several times before Marcus felt satisfied.

"The battle?"

"We were victorious. They didn't attack again once their volley was finished. I think it was designed to soften us up for next time."

Marcus smiled at his underling. "*You* think?"

"Oh, you haven't heard? I've been promoted to Grand Master while you were sleeping."

"Forgive me if I don't salute."

"I'll let you get away with it this time, since you're wounded."

Marcus chuckled, glancing at his shoulder. "So, what of it? What do they say?"

"They say you'll recover, but you may never have full use of your arm again."

Marcus frowned, clenching his fist. His shoulder ached with the motion, but he could see no reason for such pessimism. "Explain."

"I'm a soldier, not a surgeon. Apparently, you'll be able to move it without any problem, but may not regain your full strength. And it may always hurt."

Footfalls with purpose approached, and Simon glanced toward the sound, bowing out of sight.

"So, you survived!"

Marcus smiled at Sir Guillaume de Beaujeu, Grand Master of the Knights Templar, and a good friend. "As did you."

Guillaume stood beside him with a concerned smile. "Aye, I did, though too many didn't. If we continue to suffer losses like this, we just might have to invite our sergeants to become knights!"

Marcus lifted his head up, finding Simon. "I was led to believe mine had already been promoted."

Simon snorted, scurrying out of sight, leaving Marcus and the Grand Master to roar with laughter.

Guillaume became serious, motioning toward the bandaged shoulder. "I understand you'll live, but won't be able to fight."

"It'll take more than a Saracen's arrow to keep me out of the fight, sir."

Guillaume shook his head. "No, I think your time has come"—he raised a finger to cut off Marcus' protest—"and perhaps none too soon."

"What do you mean?"

Guillaume pulled out a piece of paper. "I have word from your sister Nicoline."

Marcus tensed at the mention of the only family he had in the world, his parents long dead. "What is it? Is she all right?"

Guillaume sighed, bowing his head slightly. "I'm afraid the news isn't good."

De Claret Residence
Outside Paris, Kingdom of France
Four months later

"This is the last time I will intervene on your behalf. Understood?"

Sir Bernard de Claret bowed his head. "Yes, Father."

"It's long past time you became a man and fought your own battles. I'm sick and tired of hearing the whispers of your latest folly at dinner parties, or worse, at the Palace. You are an embarrassment to this family, and always have been. If you do not distinguish yourself in this undertaking, I will send you to Rouen to tend our lands there. At least if you embarrass yourself, word of it will most likely not reach the ears of those whose opinions matter."

"Yes, Father." Bernard's cheeks burned, as did his ears. He should have been used to it by now, the constant berating, but how could he? This was his own father chastising him, and once again doing it in front of his brothers and sister. He knew he was the laughing stock of the family, and of the aristocracy.

But it wasn't his fault. He was just awkward. He always had been, especially in his youth. And that awkwardness had made him painfully shy, and by extension, made him appear cowardly.

None of these valued traits in today's France.

He had no prospects for marriage, as no one would have him for a husband—something he couldn't blame the women with whom arrangements

14

had been made to meet. All had no doubt gone home at the end of the evening, begging their fathers to not force him upon them, and all had agreed so far, despite how powerful a man his father was.

There were others as powerful, or nearly as powerful, with sons considered catches.

He could never be mistaken for that.

His father was right. This new assignment granted him was his last opportunity. He had been assigned to the King's Personal Guard, a prestigious position for a young man, and not only that, had been placed on assignment with the leader of the unit, Sir Valentin de Vaux, to be his second-in-command on an important mission.

If he could just not bungle this assignment, he might salvage some modicum of respect from his father, and perhaps others as well.

He had been practicing. His sister Bridgett was a Godsend, helping him practice speaking with confidence, with dancing, with walking and even standing like a gentleman. He was getting better, though confidence in the presence of one's sister rarely translated into the real world.

And his father's belittling did nothing to help.

He glanced over at Bridgett, tears staining her cheeks as her older brother was yet again humiliated.

His father handed him a piece of paper. "These are your orders. Rendezvous with Sir Valentin as quickly as possible, and present him with this."

Bernard took the paper and bowed. "Yes, Father."

"And if you screw up, don't bother coming home."

"Father!" cried Bridgett, rushing from her chair toward her brother. "How could you say such a thing?"

Bernard's chest burned and his throat became tight as he fought the tears that demanded release. His sister held him tight, glaring at his father to no effect.

"You're just a little girl. You have no possible understanding of what is going on here. Now go to your room!"

"No! Not until you tell Bernard that you didn't mean what you said!"

His father raised his hand to smack her and Bernard turned Bridgett away, placing himself between her and his father. "You will *not* hit her." He surprised himself at the firmness of his tone.

And apparently his father as well. His father stared at him for a moment, a slight smile appearing. "Interesting. I do believe that's the first time you've ever shown me any sign there might be a man lurking within that pitiful shell." He jabbed a finger against Bernard's chest. "Show that attitude to Sir Valentin and the others, and you just may impress them enough to salvage your sad existence."

His father turned on his heel and left the room, leaving his brothers snickering, his mother mute with her chin buried in her chest and her shoulders rolled forward, and Bridgett facing him, her eyes wide with pride.

"I know you'll do brilliantly, Brother."

Bernard smiled slightly. "I-I hope so, Sister."

For if he didn't, there would be no point in living.

Crécy-la-Chapelle, Kingdom of France

"This is your uncle, Sir Marcus."

The two small children stared up at him, wide-eyed with fear. He didn't blame them. He must be quite the sight. Two decades in the harsh climate of the Holy Land took its toll, compounded by the countless scars from countless battles marring his face and hands.

He put on his best smile. "So you must be my nephew, Jacques, that I have heard so much about."

Jacques bowed slightly. "Y-yes, sir."

"And you, little one, must be my niece, Angeline."

She curtsied before hiding behind her slightly larger brother.

"Well children, don't you have anything to say to your uncle?"

The two children stared at Mrs. Leblanc, confused. It had taken Marcus and his entourage almost four months to reach home, travel from the Holy Land difficult at the best of times. As a Templar favored by the Grand Master, his trip was much shorter than most, but it hadn't been fast enough.

His sister was dead.

Nicoline's letter had begged him to return before she fell prey to the disease ravaging her body. According to Mrs. Leblanc, she had held on for months in the hopes he would return, but had succumbed before the letter had even arrived.

He had wept privately when told, then visited the grave before seeing the children left behind, parentless, their father having died two years ago

17

saving young Angeline from drowning. Marcus had prayed for hours at his sister's grave, begging her for forgiveness, for not being there for her.

You should have returned when Henri died.

He had been selfish. He enjoyed his life as a Templar. It gave him purpose, and respect, things he remembered having little of before joining. He loved his brothers, he loved his Lord, and he loved his way of life. Though the worldly pleasures were few, he needed little beyond the camaraderie the Order gave him. He didn't need women or drink, possessions or lands. He only needed the Order.

Or so he had thought.

It wasn't until he faced the prospect of losing his sister that he realized how just knowing she was out there had been an anchor to his home, to his family. He hadn't seen her in twenty years, and his only memories of her were as a girl of twelve. Though they didn't see each other, she wrote him constantly, and he her when possible, though not as frequently as he knew she would like. He lived her life through those letters, rejoicing in her marriage and the birth of her two children, weeping as his mother died of influenza, and his father months later of a broken heart.

He was all that remained of his family.

"Are you our Uncle Marcus, the Templar Knight?"

He snapped out of his self-pity, staring at little Angeline, peeking out from behind her brother. "Yes. Did your mother speak of me?"

She nodded.

"What did she say?"

Shrugged shoulders.

He smiled. "I hope she said nice things."

18

Her eyes widened. "*Very* nice things. She said you were the best brother a girl could have!"

Marcus laughed. "Well, I'm sure your brother is just as good."

"No he's not! He pinches me all the time!"

Marcus gave Jacques a look of mock disapproval. "Is this true?"

The boy hung his head in shame. "Yes, Uncle."

"Well, that stops now, understood?"

"Yes, Uncle." His shoulders shook, tears erupting. He was quickly joined by his sister. Marcus stared at them, mouth agape, unsure of what to do. He turned to Mrs. Leblanc, helpless. She leaped into action, corralling the two sobbing children into the next room, gently cooing at them. She returned a moment later, the sobs still heard, though settling.

Marcus looked at her sheepishly. "Umm, I'm sorry about that."

She batted a hand at him. "They're children, and they just lost their mother. They'll be irrational like that for months. You'll just have to get used to it."

His chest tightened at her last statement. He had come to see his dying sister, and had to admit that during his entire journey, it had never occurred to him that she might actually die. His only thoughts of the children were that he hoped they didn't lose their mother.

But they had.

"The children seem to have taken a liking to you."

Mrs. Leblanc smiled, staring at the doorway she had led them through. "Yes, they are precious. Very well behaved." She turned to him. "A credit to your sister."

19

He bowed slightly. "Thank you. I'm afraid, though, I barely knew my sister. I left when she was only twelve."

Her head bobbed slowly. "Yes, I know. It was her one regret in life that she didn't get to see you again, to see what kind of man you had become." She stared him up and down. "A fine man, I think." She pointed toward his white surcoat, the red cross of the Templars prominently displayed. "And a fine calling you have committed yourself to."

He bowed slightly deeper. "Thank you, ma'am."

"But now you have a greater responsibility."

He sucked in a slow, deep breath. "The children."

"Yes, the children. They need a home, and they need a father."

"They have, or rather, had, a father."

"A father they barely remember. They need someone in their life to guide them."

He stared at the wall separating them from the children, two little shadows stretching across the floor from the sun pouring in a window beyond, revealing two young eavesdroppers at the door. "You seemed to be a fine guide."

The woman waved her hands in front of herself vigorously, shaking her head. "Absolutely not! I'm too old for young ones, and I'm not family. I took them in as a favor to your sister, because she was a good friend and good neighbor, and it was the Christian thing to do, but my responsibility ended the moment you arrived. This is your home now, and these are your children to deal with. I will help you, of course, but their responsibility must be yours."

Marcus' heart hammered, the blood pulsing

through his ears almost overwhelming. He couldn't imagine raising children. He wasn't a father. He wasn't even much of a brother. He was a soldier, and a good one at that.

There had to be an alternative.

"The Church? Perhaps they could take them?"

Mrs. Leblanc stared at him aghast, her eyes wide, her mouth agape. "Your sister would roll over in her grave if she heard you suggest such a thing!"

Jacques erupted from his perch behind the door, tears flowing, his cheeks flushed. "Please don't send us away!" He slammed into Mrs. Leblanc, hugging her legs, Angeline following a moment later, mimicking the display.

His chainmail suddenly felt tight, heavier than usual. His cheeks burned, his chest heaved, and the world closed in on him as the wails of the children continued. He stared at Mrs. Leblanc, barely able to focus. "I-I'll be back."

He beat a hasty retreat, the first time he had ever done so, twenty years of victorious soldiering wiped away by two distraught children. He burst through the door and nearly ran into his sergeant and squires, relaxing near the horses.

"Sir, are you all right?" asked his sergeant, Simon.

"Get this off me!" he gasped, grasping at his chainmail. His squires leaped forward, removing the constrictive armor, useless against the onslaught of the enemy he now faced. He collapsed to his knees, clasping his hands behind his neck as he tried to open his lungs as wide as he could, still having difficulty breathing.

Simon knelt in front of him. "Sir, what's wrong?"

21

Marcus closed his eyes, forcing himself to breathe in a steady, slow rhythm, his pounding heart finally settling. He looked at Simon, his sergeant, his friend. "What would you do if you found out your life was over, and you could no longer be a Templar?"

"I'd get drunk."

Marcus extended a hand. "Help me up, then find me a tavern."

Simon rose, pulling his master to his feet. "Sir? Your oath!"

"Is no longer of any matter." He stared at the house, then the farm surrounding it. "Today, I am no longer a soldier, no longer a knight. I am but a lowly farmer."

Outside Coulommiers, Kingdom of France

"Here they come," hissed Sir Valentin de Vaux's second-in-command, Sir Bernard de Claret. Valentin nodded, shifting slightly to his right to get a better view of the small group of travelers now emerging from the forest. They were all on horseback, even the squires, suggesting to those not in the know, that these men approaching were of some importance.

But he was in the know.

And they were.

Yet it didn't matter.

They were going to die.

He raised his arm, the signal picked up to his left and right by the others already in position for the ambush, then rapidly lowered it. A flurry of arrows sliced through the air, only the best archers selected for this most important of missions. The squires fell first, then the horses of the knights and their sergeants, their whinnies of agony ignored, the death of the noble beasts of no concern to him.

He only cared about their invaluable cargo.

He swept his hand forward, and dozens of men streamed from the surrounding trees, quickly encircling the survivors as he strode calmly from his position, flanked by Bernard and his sergeant. His men surrounding their prey parted for him, and he smiled as he found the three knights and their respective sergeants in the middle, backs to each other, swords drawn.

"What is the meaning of this?" demanded the

eldest and most senior. "Do you not see our surcoats? Do you not know who we are?"

Valentin approached him, keeping enough distance that any move toward him wouldn't beat the arrow of one of the archers mixed among his men. "Who you are, is of no importance to us. What you carry on your person, is."

The man's eyes narrowed as they came to rest on Valentin. "Of what do you speak?"

"You have a document in your possession. I want it."

The man glanced toward his dying horse, returning his glare to Valentin. "I have many documents, none of which are yours to have. Now be off with you, or the King shall hear of your crimes!"

A smile spread across Valentin's face as he removed his cloak, revealing the crest on his surcoat. "You fool. Who do you think sent me?" He turned on his heel and nodded, a dozen arrows loosed.

Crécy-la-Chapelle, Kingdom of France

"Sir, are you sure you want another?"

Sir Marcus slapped his sergeant on the back, then grabbed the barmaid by the waist, drawing her closer. "I've only just begun!"

She laughed as she gently extricated herself. "I'll take that as a yes to another round." As she made her way to the bar, Marcus couldn't help but stare at her ample bottom, the stirring in his loins impossible to ignore.

"She's a fine looking woman, that one."

Simon nodded. "She is that. But she's not for you, sir."

Marcus frowned at his sergeant, emptying the last of his wine. "But you forget, good man, that I am no longer a Templar, no longer bound by my oath to a pious life." He stared appreciatively at the barmaid's mighty bosom as she returned with four more cups. "Tonight, I want to get drunk, and lie with a beautiful woman." He tore his eyes away from her exposed flesh and stared up at her. "Interested?"

She gave him a look. "With the amount you've had? I'd rather go home to my husband and be disappointed there!"

The tavern roared with laughter, and Marcus had no idea why, feeling a flash of anger rush through him. But his entourage was laughing as well, and they would never do so if he were meant to take offense. Simon noticed his confusion and held up a finger, then bent it downward.

25

Marcus suddenly understood, tossing his head back and joining in the laughter. He lifted his mug high. "A fine woman indeed!" He drained half of it, the others doing the same, when three men entered the tavern, their surcoats indicating they were members of King Philip's Personal Guard. An uneasy silence swept across those gathered as the men headed for a table near the back, the occupants scampering away.

"I don't like the look of them," muttered Simon.

His squire David nodded. "Why would three of the King's Personal Guard be here?"

Simon shook his head. "Probably passing through."

"I'll ask them!" Marcus leaped to his feet before his men could stop him, stumbling toward the new arrivals. "You there! State your business, in the name of His Holiness, the Pope!"

The three men stared at him, two in shock, the one in the middle barely registering any notice of their interrogator. Marcus heard his men approaching from behind, but he waved them off.

"Are you deaf? I asked you a question."

The calm one stared him in the eyes. "My business is that of the King's, and therefore is no business of yours. Go away, you drunken fool, before I have you arrested, or run through."

Marcus smiled slightly, half his lip curling. "You dare threaten me?" He drew his sword slightly, the firelight shimmering off the blade he was certain had tasted more blood than that beaten by the hearts of these three men combined. "I don't think you know whom it is you are addressing, good sir."

The other two men leaped to their feet, their chairs

scattering across the floor as they reached for their swords. Simon and the others surged forward as Marcus continued his staring contest with the third man, still seated.

He slowly rose, waving off his men, Marcus' entourage lowering their weapons slightly. "We have business to attend to, and no time for this." He rounded the table, stopping only inches from Marcus' nose. "You are fortunate, old man, otherwise your numbered days would have ended tonight."

The man strode with purpose from the tavern, his companions rushing after him, as Marcus drained the rest of his drink.

And passed out.

"Could they be a problem?"

Sir Valentin mounted his horse and urged it toward their camp outside of the village. He glanced at his new second-in-command, Sir Bernard, as he came up beside him. "One Templar Knight, a sergeant, and two squires? Hardly."

Yet he wasn't as certain as he made it sound. Why were they here? Asking the locals could raise suspicions, and he couldn't risk that. Besides, there was no time. Their business here would be conducted in two days, and there was no delaying that. They had a schedule to keep, and it was tight.

"Should we postpone? Perhaps leave this one until later, after they've left?"

Valentin shook his head. "We have no way of knowing when they're leaving. And should our target catch word of what is happening, he might go into hiding, and we may never find him." He exhaled loudly, shaking his head. "No, we must stick to our schedule."

His sergeant came up the other side. "I thought Templars didn't drink."

Valentin chewed his cheek for a moment. While it was true Templars weren't supposed to overindulge, he had seen it on occasion, and like all good Christians that sinned, they went to confession and did their penance. He had no doubt this man would do the same. Something had caused him to drink, and he was clearly inexperienced at it. His loyal men had tried to stop him from making a fool of himself, though they had failed miserably. He was fortunate it hadn't turned into a fight, as the attention it would have brought could have scuttled their mission.

And failing the King wasn't an option.

Four Templars, here, of all places.

Why?

Why were they here?

He desperately needed an answer to this question. Could their business here somehow interfere with his? And if so, did the Templars know of what was happening?

Impossible!

There was no way they could know. It was too soon. The raid on the convoy had taken place only this morning, and there had been no witnesses. They had already buried the bodies, and their surcoats, along with anything else that might have identified them as Templars, had been hidden miles from the graves.

If either burial site were discovered, neither could point back to him or his men, and there was almost no

28

chance of both being discovered.

They were safe.

For now.

Yet none of that answered the question of why these four men were here, on this night, in this village. He had never been here before in his life, and after his mission was complete, never would be again. No Templars were supposed to be stationed here. They could be passing through, though Templars weren't known for setting themselves up at the local tavern.

No, they were here for some other reason.

"We'll have to watch for them. Experienced soldiers could be a problem."

Bernard agreed. "Should we bring more men?"

"No, that could draw too much attention. Three is already too many, though any fewer risks failure." A thought suddenly occurred to him, and a smile slowly spread. Bernard noticed.

"What has you so pleased?"

Valentin turned toward his second-in-command. "I just had an idea."

Bernard grinned. "A devious one, by the looks of it."

Valentin's smile widened. "You have no idea."

De Rancourt Farm
Crécy-la-Chapelle, Kingdom of France

"My place is at your side."

Sir Marcus shook his head at his good friend and sergeant. "Simon, your place is with the Order, in the Holy Land. You know that as well as I."

"If mine is, then so is yours."

"You know that isn't possible."

"Why?"

Marcus glanced over his shoulder, Jacques playing fetch with a mastiff that outweighed the boy two-to-one, while little Angeline hung laundry with Mrs. Leblanc. "You know why."

"Yes, and it is a noble undertaking. You have agreed to be a father to these children in need. To raise them as your sister would want you to, so that they never know the horrors of the orphanage. It is an honorable thing you are doing, but you will need help."

"I need a woman to be their mother." Marcus eyed Simon up and down. "You don't fit the part."

Simon laughed, the others snickering. He curtsied. "Are you so sure?"

Marcus roared with laughter, the small farm coming to a halt for a moment before activities resumed. "I will miss your sense of humor."

"No, you won't, because I'm staying. If you are to work this farm, you will need help. I'm almost as old as you, and my best days are behind me. It would be my honor to serve you one more time."

Marcus stared at his friend, his chest tightening at the loyalty displayed. Simon was a good friend. His best. They had served together for more years than either probably cared to count, and a bond had formed under battle, and in brotherhood among the Order, that until this moment, he hadn't realized how unbreakable. He sighed. "If you want to shovel pig dung and plant crops, then who am I to say no?"

"I will stay as well, sir."

"As will I."

Marcus turned toward his two young squires, though as he stared at them, he realized that they too weren't young anymore. He looked at the youngest, Jeremy, who had to be thirty if he were a day, and David was at least another five years older. They had served him for years, and though their station meant there was an official distance between them, he considered them friends.

He rose, holding his arms out, and his men drew closer. "The four of us, farmers." He tossed his head back, laughing once more as he stared up at the heavens. "Lord, I would never have dreamt that this was the path you had laid out for us." He lowered his gaze, smiling from man to man, staring into the eyes of each, searching for any hint that they were doing this out of some sense of perceived duty, seeking any hint of hesitation behind their words.

And he found none.

"Then it is settled. I will seek out the Order's local commander, and inform him of our decision tomorrow."

Something poked his bum, pushing up. He spun

around to find the mastiff standing there, an invasive nose sniffing at his crotch. Marcus pushed the beast's head aside. "I'm not about to have the first thing to sniff around there in a lifetime be a dog!"

Simon slapped him on the shoulder. "I think that barmaid was taking a liking to you. Maybe if you keep at it, she'll be sniffing down there before you know it!"

Marcus chuckled as he dropped to a knee, taking the mastiff's head in his hands and scratching behind its ears. "So, what's your name?"

"Tanya."

Marcus leaned to the side slightly so he could see past the dog that probably outweighed his squires. "What was that?"

Angeline took a step forward. "Tanya. Her name is Tanya."

"Ahh, from the Latin for princess." He stared Tanya in the eyes. "Are you a princess?" The dog snorted. "Sounds like any princess I've ever met." His men roared. He patted her on her side with a good thump. "A fine beast. She seems friendly."

Mrs. Leblanc rushed over. "Oh, be careful with that one! She'll tear off your arm if you're not careful." She paused as Tanya rolled onto her side, presenting her stomach for a scratch.

"Sir, I think you finally have a woman in your life," muttered Simon, the others stifling their laughs unsuccessfully.

Marcus scratched the dog's belly. "Oh, she seems pretty friendly."

Mrs. Leblanc scratched the back of her neck. "Well, I'll be…I've never seen her so friendly with anyone except the boy and his father, God rest his soul."

Marcus rose, and Tanya flipped back over, taking up a position beside him. Marcus scratched behind her ears once again. "Well, I think having her around will be helpful. A good dog is worth his weight in gold for warning of danger."

Mrs. Leblanc laughed. "Oh, you soldiers, always thinking of danger. Nothing ever happens in this godforsaken town. The only thing she's good for is keeping the rats and predators away." She smiled as Tanya pressed her snout into Marcus' hand. "I think she's found her new master."

Marcus looked down at the dog then over at young Jacques, whose sad, drooping eyes suggested he wasn't at all pleased with this turn of events. Marcus snapped his fingers and Tanya stared up at him. "Go play with Jacques," he said, pointing at the boy. The dog continued to stare at him for a moment, then leaped toward Jacques, the two of them running behind the house, giggles once again filling the air.

"That boy has needed a father these past two years." Mrs. Leblanc wiped a tear from her cheek. "And I dare say he's found one."

Marcus sighed.

I wouldn't be so sure of that.

De Rancourt Farm
Crécy-la-Chapelle, Kingdom of France

Sir Marcus tossed and turned in the too soft bed of his sister. For two decades, he had slept on a simple bedroll, often on the dirt. And though he had often dreamed of a soft bed to curl up in and sleep for a month, now that his dreams had come true, it was a genuinely horrible experience.

His back was killing him.

You'll get used to it.

He rolled over and stared out the window, a heavy rain drenching the humble farm. His family was nobility, though distant, which meant they were never wealthy. But it did mean he could become a knight, which was all he had dreamed about as a boy.

His father had been a knight, though of little prestige—he wasn't very good at it. He had been wounded in the Crusades, apparently in his first battle, forcing his return, much of the family wealth, such as it was, spent. Marcus had thought it humiliating as a naïve child, and had been determined to do better, selfishly leaving his family to fend for themselves as soon as he could.

He had no idea how hard it would be for his sister after their father's passing. Fortunately, she was still nobility, and eventually a widowed nobleman, relatively poor though not as much so as his sister, took a liking to her, and she him, and they had married—but not before a decade of struggle, a struggle he regretted every moment of every day.

Yet she had survived, and this proud though humble home was a testament to her spirit, this farm a monument to a family's ethic, and the children sleeping in the next room what remained of their love.

Thunder rocked the small home, the view from the window flickering a moment later, the barn where his men slept silhouetted against the momentarily bright sky.

I'd rather be with them.

He wasn't sure how this would work. He had to stay in the home for the children's sake, and there wasn't room for another three full-sized men to also bed down here. He was moved that they had insisted on staying with him. Loyalty like that was rare in his experience, especially outside the Order. The bond formed on the field of battle, and on your knees in prayer, were unlike anything most could imagine.

And he'd give anything to be out in that chilly barn, on the hard ground, surrounded by the men he called brothers.

Another clap of thunder rattled the windows, and Angeline shrieked. Little footsteps pounded the floor moments later, followed by a hammering on his door.

"Come in."

The door opened and Angeline stepped inside, the tears staining her cheeks reflected from the light flickering through his window. "Can I sleep with you?"

His eyes widened. He wasn't sure what to do. What would his sister have said?

She would have said 'yes,' you heartless fool!

He shuffled closer to the wall. "Get in. But don't make a habit of it."

35

She bolted from the doorway, leaping in the bed and shoving her tiny legs under the covers. He was about to tell her to go close the door when Jacques appeared.

"Let me guess, you want to sleep in here as well?"

Jacques looked about, avoiding eye contact, then rushed to the bed at another clap of thunder.

"Close the door."

Jacques hesitated at the prospect of leaving the safety of the bed, but complied, bolting for the door, closing it, then returning at an equally blistering pace. Marcus rolled over, putting his back to the children and his front toward the wall with the window, then closed his eyes. A set of tiny knees dug into his back as Angeline pressed her petite body against his, her forehead tight against his shoulders. Moments later the bed moved as Jacques shifted closer as well, a hand slapping onto Marcus' tender shoulder.

He winced but stifled the desire to vocalize the pain.

He lay in the darkness, the breathing of his sister's children slowly calming down, soon settling into a steady, rhythmic pace as they fell asleep, the thunder and lightning outside apparently forgotten. He closed his eyes and smiled, picturing his sister lying here instead of him, and for the first time in his life, understood the joy children must bring parents everywhere.

I promise you, Sister, that I will die before I let anything happen to them.

Fabron Residence
Crécy-la-Chapelle, Kingdom of France

Pierre Fabron galloped the small woodcarving of a horse across his bedchamber floor, making the sounds of clopping hooves with the clicking of his tongue against the roof of his mouth. The mighty beast skidded to a halt, rearing on its hind legs as he confronted the enemy.

"Halt, and identify yourself!"

But there was no reply.

Of course there was no reply.

He was alone.

As he always was.

He hated this new home. He had yet to make any friends, and with his father rather wealthy compared to others, the poor kids, who outnumbered one hundred to one those who weren't, shunned him.

All except Jacques. He was nice to him. Apparently, his family had noble blood as his did, which was a surprise since he lived on a farm that didn't have any servants working the fields.

Could noblemen be poor?

He had asked the question of his father, who had readily confirmed the possibility.

"If you are referring to the young Jacques I think you are, his father died a couple of years ago, and his mother just this year. The family is of noble blood, but it is distant. It allows the sons to become knights, but little else. Being a knight is expensive, so for many, it simply isn't an option." He had looked at him over his dinner. "There is no shame in being a farmer." He tapped his plate with his knife. "Without them, we wouldn't have such wonderful food to eat."

A nobleman too poor to be a knight. It was a shocking concept to him, but then, he had never really known what poverty was. His family wasn't rich, though they definitely weren't poor. His father was well educated, and worked for the King as an auditor, moving from one town to the next after affairs had been put in order.

Though this town was poorer than most, with few other officials with children his age.

Which left him with his toys.

And his imagination, an imagination failing him today.

Three hard raps on the front door had him leaping to his feet and eagerly pressing an eye against a knot in the door that let him see through to the front entrance.

His mother opened the door and gasped, stepping back, two large men entering before she could say anything.

"Is Mr. Guy Fabron here?"

"I am he. Who are you? What do you want?"

Pierre could hear something in his father's voice that he recognized, though had never heard from the only man he had ever really known. He had only heard it in his own voice, that of a child.

It was fear.

"Do you recognize this document?"

A piece of paper was held up by the man doing the talking, Pierre only able to see him from the side. His father stepped into view. "Of course. What of—" His father paused, his jaw dropping. "Wait a moment, how did you get this?" He stared at the man. "Who are you?"

"How we have come into possession of this document, is none of your concern, and who we are should be obvious to you. Now"—the man stepped closer to Pierre's father—"were any other documents signed at your meeting?"

"I will *not* answer. I *cannot* answer. I swore an oath before God to not talk about anything discussed at the meeting. If you are who you purport to be, then you should understand that."

"I do. Which is why I know questioning you further is of no use."

Pierre gasped as he heard a sword drawing from a sheath. His mother screamed and he slapped his hands over his mouth as the man stepped back, his sword swinging in a wide arc as his father retreated, pushing his mother out of the way. The blade sliced through the air, and for a moment, Pierre thought it had missed, a sigh of relief escaping, when his mouth filled with bile as a bright red stain spread quickly across his father's shirt. His father fell to his knees, reaching forward, grabbing the man's surcoat.

A boot unceremoniously shoved him to his back as the attacker flipped his sword, hilt toward the ceiling, changing his grip so that both hands now clasped around the handle.

Then the sword plunged through his father's chest.

His mother screamed, and the forgotten woodcarving fell to the floor with a thud. The murderer pulled his sword from his father's body, then turned toward the sound, giving Pierre a clear view of the bright white surcoat with red cross emblazoned on the front.

Templars!

The man pointed toward his bedchamber door. "Check it out." The other man strode toward his room and Pierre retreated, his head on a swivel as he tried to find a place to hide. "Shut up!" His mother's screams became muffled, then he heard a cry of pain, and something hit the hard floor.

Mama!

He turned and saw the gaping maw where the monsters lived, the monsters under his bed.

It was dark, and surely no one would dare look there.

He grabbed his pillow then scampered under the bed and into the corner as far as he could, pulling the pillow behind him as the door opened. He drew the pillow tight, hiding as much of his body as he could behind it, as the footfalls of heavy boots approached the bed.

"Someone's coming!"

Pierre held his breath as the boots stopped in front of his bed. He heard a grunt, and the bed lifted from the far end, up off the floor, the shaft of light rapidly approaching as his eyes bulged.

"Let's go. Now!"

The man grumbled, dropping the bed to the floor with an unholy rattle, the footfalls rapidly receding, the front door slamming shut only moments later. Pierre remained in the corner, gripping his pillow tight, as horses outside whinnied then galloped away.

He wasn't sure how long he remained there,

trembling, but it was long enough to soil himself, though when he finally realized he had done so, he couldn't be sure of when it had happened.

All he knew was his cheeks burned, and his clothes were uncomfortably, embarrassingly, damp.

He climbed out from under the bed and quickly changed his clothes, determined no one would witness his shame, then tentatively stepped out of his bedroom. His father lay near the door, his mother only paces away, both lying in pools of blood. A whimper escaped, and his shoulders shook as he was suddenly overcome with sobs. He dropped to his knees, between the bodies of his parents, unsure of whom to go to first, whom to grieve for first, as any choice was a betrayal to the other.

He grabbed his mother's hand, then stretched out his other, through the blood, his body now prone on the floor as he reached for the outstretched hand of his father. He grunted, grasping at his father's arm, finally clasping his fingers, squeezing his tiny hand around them as his cheek collapsed into the blood of his father, or his mother.

Whose it was, he didn't know, nor care.

They were gone, and he was alone, in a town where nobody knew them.

He closed his eyes and prayed, wondering why Templars would kill his parents in cold blood.

Templar Commandry
Coulommiers, Kingdom of France

"And you swear to maintain your vows?"

Sir Marcus nodded at Sir Raimond de Comps, the Templar commander for the region. Marcus had been delighted to discover the man he was to meet was Raimond, the two having met in the Holy Land on several occasions, the reunion a joyful one. "I swear it."

"There's a rumor going about that a Templar Knight was seen drunk at a tavern in Crécy-la-Chapelle, and that he challenged three of the King's Personal Guard to a fight."

Marcus' cheeks flushed. "You heard about that?"

"Everyone has heard about that. It is fortunate that whoever this man was, he passed out before he could remove his sword from its scabbard."

Marcus glanced over his shoulder at Simon, who quickly stared at the floor. "I had been told there was a glorious battle in which this drunkard bested three of the King's finest."

"Your sources appear questionable."

"Indeed."

"Umm, I'm going to wait outside," murmured Simon.

Raimond smiled as Simon quickly departed. "Your men's loyalty is a testament to your character."

Marcus bowed slightly. "Our Lord has blessed me with the finest of companions."

"And they wish to remain at your side?"

"To a man."

"Well, their oaths are not as binding nor restrictive as yours, of course, and I see no reason to deny them their wish. But as long as they wear the symbols of our Order, they are to conduct themselves as they would were they not farmers tending their fields."

"I am confident they will agree to these expectations."

Raimond drew a deep breath then sighed loudly. "Are you certain this is what you want?"

Marcus frowned. "I would be lying if I said I didn't have doubts, but I know it is what my sister would want, and I have seen too many orphans to know that I cannot allow such a thing to happen to my niece and nephew."

"You are a good man, Sir Marcus, a good Christian."

Marcus bowed deeply. "You humble me, sir."

Raimond drew closer, lowering his voice. "I must confess, I am pleased you and your men are here. More loyal men in the region, I believe, is a good thing at this time."

"Is something wrong?"

Raimond shook his head. "I don't know. More of the King's men have been sighted in the area, and several of our Order have reported being harassed when alone, by people posing as townsfolk, yet who bore scars that suggested they were anything but."

"It's been long known the King and His Holiness have been at odds. Do you think he's making a play against the Church, and those who would defend it?"

Raimond grunted. "Nothing would surprise me

43

with that man, however, to move against Rome?" He sighed. "If anyone could, if anyone *would*, it would be King Philip."

"And should such a thing happen?"

"Then the Order must defend the interests of the Church, as we have sworn to do."

"That could mean war."

"It could. In fact, the Grand Master is so concerned, he's sent representatives from the Holy Land. Also, a contingent of our Order is escorting a delegation from Rome to meet with the King in an attempt to calm things."

"When will they arrive?"

"The delegation should be arriving in Paris any day now. Our representatives from the Holy Land were to have arrived yesterday, according to a messenger that arrived earlier in the week, but they are late."

Marcus frowned, staring at Raimond. "You seem concerned."

"I am. Frankly, I shouldn't be, as being late by a day means little, but something tells me my concerns are justified. The messenger told me they called a meeting not even a week ago, with others from the Order, most of the senior representatives in the area, as well as influential nobility known to be sympathetic to our Order rather than the King. There should be little reason for our men to be late, but a meeting such as this, could be considered treasonous by a suspicious king."

Marcus' head bobbed slowly as he considered Raimond's words. "I must admit, I'm surprised our men would hold such a meeting given these tensions."

"I can understand their reasoning. They have been

44

journeying for months. I would assume this meeting was an attempt to get a sense of the current state of affairs, and those invited would be best able to inform them, with little risk to the King finding out. And since this was a diplomatic mission, frankly, it is a meeting even I would conduct, and shouldn't be considered unusual."

"Though if one were looking for conspiracies and conspirators…"

Raimond sighed. "Hence my fears."

"If this meeting were attended by those truly loyal to the Templars, I wouldn't fear, but too often it has been my experience that those who purport to be one thing publicly, then in private another, too often turn out to be spies, or double-agents. Our men could have been betrayed by one of those who attended."

Raimond paled slightly. "Now *you* have me worried. I must admit, there is very little intrigue in these parts compared to the Holy Land where you have spent most of your life, so I will bow to your experience. What do you think we should do?"

Marcus chewed his cheek for a moment, staring at his well-worn boots. "We need to find out what happened to our delegation from the Holy Land. They should be easy to find if we trace their expected route. And I would find out who was at that meeting. If our men were betrayed, we need to know by whom."

Raimond closed his eyes briefly, placing a hand on Marcus' shoulder. "Thank the good Lord you are here. Without your counsel, I don't know what I'd do."

"Do you have men who can help?"

Raimond shook his head. "There are few knights in the area. Most of our Order in these parts defend our holdings, or have left for the Crusade."

"Then I offer my services."

Raimond smiled broadly. "I had hoped you would. And I have an idea on where you can start."

Fabron Residence
Crécy-la-Chapelle, Kingdom of France

Pierre heard horses and men laughing. They were nearing, the horses' hooves suggesting a slow gait. Surely those who had murdered his parents wouldn't return, and wouldn't be moving so slowly, yet he couldn't be sure. But if they were coming back, he couldn't let them find him here on the floor.

There'd be no escaping them.

He pushed to his knees, his hand slipping in the blood, causing him to fall back to the floor with a squish. More carefully this time, he rose to his feet then stepped toward the door, wiping his bloodstained hands on his shirt. He took one last look at the bodies of his parents, then opened the door slowly, peering out into the bright sun. He held up a hand to block the light, squinting as he searched for someone who might help.

But he saw no one.

And he didn't know whom to go to for help. He didn't know any of his neighbors, he didn't know where any representatives of the King might live.

The voices were almost atop him now, the men sounding cheerful and friendly. A dog barked, a happy bark, coming from the same direction, as if it were one of the merry men.

He had to take a chance.

He stepped through the door, then, as if they had a mind of their own, his little legs propelled him into the street and toward the men on horseback. As he

47

neared, he questioned his decision, but it was too late.

They were already directly in front of him, the dog, easily his size, snorted at him, though didn't attack.

He stopped, looking up at the man who appeared to be the leader of these four riders, his bearded face worn and scarred. The man leaned forward in his saddle.

"What is it, boy? Are you all right?"

Pierre stared at him, then noticed something, finally tearing his eyes away from the man's face and focusing on his surcoat.

A bright white surcoat, with a large red cross emblazoned upon it.

The symbol of the Knights Templar.

And the same symbol worn by those who had murdered his family.

The world suddenly became dark as his heart slammed and his pulse pounded in his ears. His knees gave out, and he never felt himself hit the muddy road.

Sir Marcus leaped from his horse and rushed to the boy's side, Tanya already sniffing at the prone child. The others gathered around, covering their master in case danger was near.

"Is that blood?" asked Simon, but the question was redundant. They had all seen enough in battle to know exactly what was covering the boy from almost head to toe.

Marcus quickly examined the boy for wounds, finding none. "It isn't his." He held out a hand. "Water."

A canteen was thrust into his hand moments later, and he poured some of the cool liquid onto the boy's lips, eliciting a moan.

"Sir, we have company."

He continued administering to the boy, his sergeant's tone not indicating any danger. "Locals?"

"Yes, sir."

Marcus looked up to see about a dozen villagers emerging from their homes and businesses, gathering around the excitement, though keeping a wary distance, his men a menacing sight to those not familiar with war. "Does anyone know who this boy is?"

An elderly man stepped forward, a bony finger extended toward the house they had seen him emerge from. "I believe he's the auditor's boy. Pierre, I think. They just arrived a couple of weeks ago, so I'm not certain."

"Is he dead?" asked a woman from behind them.

Marcus shook his head. "No." The boy coughed and opened his eyes. He stared into Marcus' face, then his gaze drifted back to the surcoat. He pushed away, but Marcus held his arm. "What is it boy, why are you so afraid of me?"

Pierre pointed at Marcus' chest. Marcus glanced down at the almost forgotten surcoat, and placed a hand on the cross. "Is it this?"

The boy nodded.

"Do you know what this represents?" The boy said nothing, but his head bobbed slightly. "Then you know it means I'm a Templar Knight. It means I'm sworn to protect people like you. What makes you so afraid of it?"

The boy closed his eyes then finally opened them, staring at Marcus. "The men who killed my mama and papa were Templars like you."

Marcus' jaw dropped and he stared up at the others, all in as much shock as he was at the boy's statement. He stood the boy up and took a knee, staring into his eyes. "What makes you think they were Templars like me?"

The boy pressed a bloody finger against the Templar cross. "They wore these."

Marcus frowned. He could detect no deceit in the boy's voice, and it was his opinion Pierre was telling him the truth.

Or at least his version of the truth.

He had learned long ago there were three sides to every story, the important one, the truth, usually lying somewhere between the others. And there was no way Templars murdering this young boy's parents was the truth.

He tapped the red cross on his surcoat. "Are you sure it was red and not black?"

"Yes."

"Well, you have nothing to fear from me and my men, understood?"

He nodded.

"Good. Now, how about I go find out what happened?"

Again, the boy nodded.

Marcus stood, staring at the crowd. "Can someone watch the boy while we check on his parents?"

A woman stepped forward, holding out her hand toward Pierre. "I'll watch him. I know—knew—his mother."

Marcus motioned toward the woman. "Go with

her."

The boy shook his head. "No, I want to go with you."

Marcus sighed, unfamiliar with how to deal with children. He decided to treat him as a new recruit. "Fine, but you do what I say, understood?"

"Yes, sir."

"Good." Marcus grabbed the reins of his horse and headed for the boy's home, Tanya beside Pierre as if his assigned protector. They reached the front, and Marcus handed the reins to Pierre. "You watch the horses."

He nodded.

Marcus pointed at Tanya. "Stay with the boy."

The dog barked and dropped to her haunches beside young Pierre, a crowd of at least two dozen now gathered. Marcus turned to them. "Everybody, please stand back, for the boy's sake."

Murmurs responded, but the crowd moved back, if only a few paces.

"Someone was standing by the window." Simon pointed at the muddy ground to the right of the entrance. Marcus stepped over and examined the ground, dozens of footprints evident, some facing the window, some away.

"He was here for some time, or there wouldn't be so many."

David glanced around. "From here he'd have a clear view of the street in both directions. Perhaps he was on watch?"

Marcus pursed his lips. "Perhaps." He pressed his boot beside one of the prints. "Small feet. Probably a shorter man."

"A woman?" asked David. "Or a boy?"

"A boy perhaps, but I can't believe a woman would be involved." Marcus stepped back and headed for the door. "Sergeant, you're with me. You two make sure nobody comes inside, especially the boy."

"Yes, sir," echoed his squires.

Marcus pushed aside the door, slightly ajar from when Pierre had fled the scene, and sighed in dismay at the sight. Two bodies lay on the floor in pools of their own blood, the man eviscerated and impaled, the woman's throat slit.

And a stain in the blood between them, in the shape of a small boy, heartbreaking.

He turned away, Simon doing the same.

"I don't know if I've ever seen a woman slain before," said his sergeant, his voice barely a whisper.

"Nor I. And to do it in one's home, where one should be safe from the dangers of the outside world." He shook his head. "Unthinkable." He drew a deep breath then forced himself to look upon the bodies once again, slowly circling them, careful not to step in any of the blood. Everything in the home was in its place, no evidence of a struggle. "Check the door. Was it forced?"

Simon stepped over to the plain wooden door and opened it, staring at the outside, then the simple latch. He closed the door, shaking his head. "It doesn't look like it was kicked open, if that's what you mean. But it's not like this is a vault. There's no lock. Anyone could have just opened it and walked in."

"We'll have to ask the boy if he remembers whether the men were invited inside, or forced their way."

"Do you really think Templars could have done this?"

"Never. Unless it was self-defense, but even then, they would stay to answer for what they were forced to do." He gestured at the scene. "And there are no weapons here. These people were unarmed. No Templar Knight would have been in any danger from these two. Especially more than one."

"How can you be sure there was more than one?"

"Because the boy said 'men,' not 'man.'"

Simon nodded. "You're far more observant than I, sir."

Marcus grunted. "It comes from two decades of keeping an eye open for Saracens intent upon plunging a blade in my back."

Simon laughed. "Thankfully, you'll find none around here."

"And let's hope it stays that way." He continued circling the bodies, and stopped near the door, his hands on his hips. "I don't think there's anything more to learn here. These people were defenseless, and were clearly murdered in cold blood. Nothing is out of order, which suggests no struggle, and if there were any perceived danger, surely the man would have sent his wife away, yet she was killed only paces from him."

"How can you be certain? Perhaps they killed her elsewhere in the house and brought her body here?"

Marcus shook his head. "No, look at the blood. There are no drag marks. No, she was killed where she now lies, as was he." He stared at the stain where the young boy had lain, the pattern suggesting he had stretched out his arms to hold both their hands, the

53

shape resembling a tiny angel connecting the two lost souls.

Heartbreaking.

"I'm going to disembowel whoever did this."

Simon grunted. "Only if you get to him before I do. There is no excuse for such barbarism."

"Especially in our name."

"That's what bothers me the most about all of this. Whoever this boy's parents were, they must have been of some importance."

Marcus stared about the home then at the man's clothes, far finer than any he had worn since joining the Order and taking his vow of poverty. "He must be a businessman of some type, or perhaps a government official. This isn't the home of a laborer."

"Didn't that old man say he was an auditor?"

Marcus nodded. "That's right."

Someone knocked on the door, and Marcus opened it to find a rotund man standing outside, hat in hand. He stared up at the much taller knight. "Are-are you Sir Marcus?"

"Yes. And you are?"

"I'm Mr. Archambault, the Bailiff's Delegate for the village. I-I understand there has been a murder?"

Marcus stepped aside. "Two."

Archambault stepped inside and gasped, making the sign of the cross. "Oh no! How horrible! Who could do such a thing?"

"If the boy is to be believed, Templars."

Archambault's eyes shot wide. "It can't be true!"

"It would appear we are in agreement. It is my belief that men impersonating Templars did this."

Archambault stepped closer to the bodies, crushing his hat against his chest as he leaned over. "Mr. and Mrs. Fabron. I had only met her once, but him, I've seen almost every day since they arrived a couple of weeks ago."

"What was his business?"

"He was an auditor for the King. He goes from town to town, determining the value of the properties in the area to assess what taxes are owed." Archambault frowned, staring at the bodies. "Not very popular, I'm afraid." He quickly turned to Marcus, fingers delicately placed over his lips. "I refer, of course, to the job, not the man. Mr. Fabron was quite delightful. A terrific sense of humor, and very fair. Most auditors I've dealt with over the years looked for any excuse to increase taxes. Why, last time, one tried to count the eggs the chickens were laying as 'prospective livestock!' Can you imagine such a thing? Just try explaining fertilization to someone who thinks a rooster is just a noisy chicken." Archambault sighed, closing his eyes for a moment. "I fear who Paris will send to replace our good Mr. Fabron. And will his replacement take revenge on our good people because of what happened to his predecessor?" Archambault suddenly reached forward, placing a hand on Marcus' arm. "Please, sir, you must figure out who did this! Not only to clear the good name of your Order, but to protect these good people from any act of retribution from the King! You must find who did this, so we can prove it wasn't us!"

Marcus looked down at the hand and it was quickly removed. "And what if it is found that someone from your town is responsible?"

Archambault firmly shook his head. "Not possible. Never will I believe someone from my home could do such a thing. I've lived with these people all my life."

"And no one new has moved here over the past while?"

Archambault shook his head. "No, no one except Mr. Fabron and his family." He paused, looking around the room, avoiding eye contact with Marcus and Simon. "And you, of course." He held up both hands, waving them in front of him. "But I, of course, don't believe you are the Templars who did this!"

"Of course."

Archambault suddenly appeared nervous. "Umm, what should I do?"

Marcus shrugged. "Do what you would normally do when you find someone dead. Notify whoever needs to be notified, then tend to the bodies."

Archambault's head bobbed viciously, nerves now ruling him. "Yes, yes, of course. How silly of me. I-I'll send word to Paris, and have the bodies taken care of." He flitted back and forth for a moment, then froze. "What of the boy?"

Marcus pursed his lips. "You'll have to contact his relatives, I guess."

"Paris will know, I suppose. But in the meantime, he'll have to stay somewhere. And I'm afraid the boy wasn't very popular."

"What do you mean?"

"Well, the son of an auditor, you know? In fact, I believe your Jacques was about the only boy he got along with."

A pit formed in Marcus' stomach.

"Could you, perhaps, take him in?"

Simon grinned at him from behind Archambault.

"You can't be serious."

"I would never be anything but in a time such as this. The boy needs a home, and from what I heard, he seems to have taken a liking to you, despite you being a Templar, and Templars—rather men posing as Templars—killing his parents."

Marcus growled slightly, briefly looking up at the heavens.

Why Lord? Why me?

He stared down at the bodies, at the two outstretched hands, as if they had tried to feel the warmth of the one they loved in their final moments.

He froze.

Something was in the man's hand. He knelt and gently pried apart the fingers, revealing a bloodied piece of cloth, only a small fragment the original white.

"What is it?" asked Archambault as he and Simon stepped closer.

Marcus rose, holding it up to the light pouring in from the open door. "I'm not sure, but it appears to be a piece of torn cloth. Perhaps from one of the attackers."

Simon leaned in. "He must have reached out and grabbed his surcoat, tearing it in the struggle."

Marcus nodded. "Perhaps."

"Is it from a Templar's surcoat?" asked Archambault.

Marcus shook his head. "Impossible to tell." He headed for the door, his chest tight, more troubled than he could recall being in a long time.

For he had just lied.

Something he rarely did.

The piece in his hand was made of a very poor quality linen cloth, a material so cheap, only knights sworn to poverty wore surcoats made from it.

Just like those first issued to him twenty years ago.

By his Templar brothers.

Outside Crécy-la-Chapelle, Kingdom of France

Sir Valentin raised a fist, bringing his men to a halt. He whistled, and his troops, hiding among the trees, appeared, one of his sergeants stepping forward.

"Success, sir?"

Valentin dismounted and carefully removed his Templar surcoat, handing it over to a waiting squire. "In a sense. One of the traitors is dead, but we are no closer to discovering what we are looking for."

"Where to next?"

"Crèvecœur-en-Brie. Another of the traitors lives there. Hopefully, he'll be more forthcoming."

"Isn't he a Templar?"

"Yes, an old one. Nothing to fear."

His sergeant spit on the ground. "I fear no Templar."

Valentin regarded him for a moment. "You should. I've seen them in battle when I served in the Holy Land. They are formidable warriors."

"Easy to be when death means nothing to you. They believe dying in battle assures them access to Heaven."

Valentin smiled slightly. "And wouldn't you die for your king?"

His sergeant squared his shoulders. "Without hesitation." He paused. "But I wouldn't expect automatic entry into Heaven for doing so. My deeds and actions should grant me that."

Valentin slapped his sergeant on the back. "You're

a good man. Now, prepare the men. We'll be leaving shortly."

"Yes, sir!"

Valentin turned to his second-in-command, Sir Bernard. "We should be there by nightfall. We'll deal with the traitor as we did his comrade."

"Are we sure there is another document?" asked Bernard.

"That is what I've been told."

"Can we trust the source?"

Valentin frowned, holding up the document summarizing the meeting held by the Templars and their supporters a week ago, pointing to the bottom corner where inscribed were the numerals three and six, with a slash between them. "Only six copies of this document were made, and the source possessed the third copy. In exchange for his life, he told me everything, and assured me another document existed."

Bernard pursed his lips. "Perhaps he was lying. We should question him again."

"Not possible. I ran him through the moment I was satisfied he had told me everything he knew."

Bernard smiled slightly. "You do have a way with people."

"I'm known for my cuddles."

His men roared with laughter, even the squires as they returned with water and rations for the weary travelers.

"Sir, I had a thought."

Valentin raised a hand. "Quiet everyone, Sir Bernard has a thought, and we don't want him to lose it!" More laughter, and Bernard flushed before finally joining in. Valentin took a bite of cheese then tore a piece of bread off with his teeth. He chewed, brushing the crumbs from his beard. "What is this thought?"

"Well, what if we can't find this other document, the one that proves these Templars and their supporters are treasonous against the King?"

"Then we will have killed a dozen men for no reason."

"But they are traitors, are they not?"

"Absolutely. Perhaps I should rephrase. We will have killed a dozen men for *good* reason, but not ultimately solved the problem these Templars pose."

"Which is what the King truly wants."

"Of course. They've been a thorn in his side, they've been a thorn in the *kingdom's* side, for decades if not longer." He held up his cup to those gathered. "The rewards will be great for all of us should we succeed!"

A roar went up among the men, men who rightfully expected to be richly rewarded for their loyalty. Valentin eyed Bernard. "Why these questions? Do you have something in mind?"

Bernard shook his head. "Umm, no, sir." He frowned, then repeated his reply under his breath. "Ah, excuse me, sir." He walked away, scratching his chin, apparently deep in thought.

A dangerous thing with that idiot.

Valentin had not been pleased to receive the new orders adding Bernard to his detail, and as second-in-command, no less. His reputation preceded him, and it wasn't good. A fool, a bumbler, a coward. He had never heard anything positive about the man, except that he was a constant source of amusement, the young ladies who had gone with him on arranged outings, telling delightful stories of his awkwardness that were the talk of the town.

How that pathetic fool could be a de Claret, I'll never know.

He turned his back on the embarrassment, returning his attention to men he had known for years, men he trusted, men he could count on in battle.

Men he could respect, and who respected him.

He might have orders to accept Bernard as his second-in-command, but those orders didn't mean he had to respect him.

Nor not kill him should the need arise.

Fabron Residence
Crécy-la-Chapelle, Kingdom of France

"What has you so troubled, sir?"

Sir Marcus led Simon and the others away from the crowd, then handed his sergeant the small piece of cloth he had recovered. "Feel this."

Simon took it, rubbing the rough cloth between his thumb and forefinger. His eyes widened and his voice lowered to a whisper. "Is this what I think it is?"

"I fear so."

"What?" asked David. Simon handed him the cloth, and David's jaw dropped. He quickly passed it to Jeremy.

"It can't be!" hissed Jeremy.

Marcus took the cloth and stuffed it into a pocket. "Four of us can't be wrong, and we are all familiar with the feel of the cloth used for our own surcoats and tunics. There can be no doubt this is that same cloth."

"Where did you find it?" asked David.

Simon frowned. "In the victim's clenched fist."

"Then he must have torn it off when he was killed." David's jaw dropped. "Could the boy be telling the truth?"

Marcus shook his head. "The boy is telling the truth, as he sees it." He patted his pocket with the piece of cloth. "This suggests that whoever killed these good people were indeed wearing Templar surcoats, but it, in my mind, in no way proves that

63

Templars actually committed this atrocity."

Simon agreed. "So whoever did it must have stolen the surcoats so they could impersonate us."

"Exactly." Marcus glanced over his shoulder at Archambault, speaking with several other town officials. "We must keep this to ourselves, at least for now. It is essential we find out who is behind this, otherwise the good name of our Order could be tarnished beyond repair."

Simon stepped slightly closer, lowering his voice further still. "What if he asks for the cloth?"

"I will make some excuse, but I don't think he will. I told him it was nothing, and he will believe that, for I am a Templar Knight." Marcus sighed. "I must go to confession soon. First drinking and cavorting with women, and now lying. I'll burn in Hell for sure should I die without having seen a priest."

Simon chuckled. "Unlikely, my friend, but I too miss their counsel. Living so far from the Holy Land makes me feel further from God than I have my entire life. It's rather unsettling."

"Agreed. When we leave here, we'll pray at the church, and ask the Lord, and the priest, for guidance. We need God in our hearts and at our side if we are to succeed."

Something poked his rear, and he turned to find Tanya panting behind him, Pierre at her side. Marcus scratched her behind the ear. "What brings you here, girl?"

Pierre stared at the ground. "Are my parents dead?"

Marcus took a knee in front him. "I'm afraid so, son."

The boy's lip trembled, but he managed to keep himself together, trying to be brave in front of the soldiers before him. Tanya pressed against the boy, as if sensing his pain. He wrapped his arms around her and closed his eyes.

Thank God for that dog.

"My father was a coward," whispered the boy, tears suddenly streaming down his face.

Marcus regarded him. "Why would you say that?"

"He was scared. I heard him. I heard it in his voice. He was scared of the men, so they killed him and my mama."

Marcus reached out and placed a hand on the boy's shoulder. "Look at me." Pierre raised his head and stared at Marcus with bloodshot eyes. "Your father was not a coward. Just because someone is scared, doesn't mean he's a coward."

"I'll bet you've never been scared."

Marcus laughed. "Son, I'm scared every time I go into battle. It's good to be scared. It gives you a rush that keeps you on edge, keeps you alert. It's God's way of heightening your senses against danger."

Pierre's eyes were wide. "*You* get scared?"

Simon stepped closer. "It's true, I've seen him nearly drop his sword once."

Marcus chuckled. "You know very well that was because my hand was covered in Saracen innards."

"Sure it was."

The squires roared with Simon, at their master's expense, even young Pierre smiling, Tanya getting excited. Marcus jerked a thumb at Jeremy. "Jeremy crapped his pants once."

Jeremy flushed red. "Umm, I thought we agreed

never to speak of it again."

Marcus grinned. "See?"

Pierre nodded, smiling.

"So, you see, if warriors like us can be scared, and we've been in battle our entire lives, you should never think less of your father for being scared. He wasn't scared of those men, he was scared of what they might do to you and your mama." He frowned. "Unfortunately, he was right to fear them, but *very* fortunately, you escaped them by being very brave."

"I just hid."

"Tell me about it."

"I heard them come in when I was in my room playing."

"So you didn't see them?"

"No, I did. Through the hole in my door."

"How many?"

"Two."

"Were they angry?"

"Not at first."

"So your father let them in?"

"My mama."

"And they were friendly at first?"

Pierre shrugged. "I think so."

"Then what happened."

"They began to argue."

"What about?"

"They showed my papa a piece of paper. He seemed angry that they had it. Then they asked him something."

"What?"

Another shrug. "I think if anything else was signed

66

at some meeting. I'm not sure. But my father wouldn't tell them anything, so they killed him, then my mama."

"Then what did they do?"

"Someone came toward my room, so I hid underneath my bed. Then someone yelled that someone was coming, so they all left. That's when I found mama and papa."

The tears threatened to begin anew.

"Would you recognize the men?"

Pierre looked away. "I-I don't know."

"You don't need to fear them, son, I'll never let anything happen to you. My men and I will protect you. You have my word."

Pierre looked at the others, all nodding, then at Marcus. "Y-you will?"

Marcus smiled. "Yes. In fact, I have agreed with the Bailiff's Delegate, Mr. Archambault, that you will come and stay at my farm with Jacques and Angeline. How does that sound?"

Pierre beamed. "That would be wonderful!"

"Good. Now, tell me, would you recognize the men?"

Pierre shrugged. "The one who killed my father, I think so. I didn't really see the other one."

"Someone yelled someone was coming. Was that from inside your home, or outside?"

"Outside."

"So then there were at least three."

"I guess."

"Good. That's more than we knew a few moments ago." Marcus smiled at Pierre. "You're a good, brave boy. Your mama and papa would be very proud of you right now."

Pierre stared at his feet.

"Now, why don't you play with Tanya for a little, while we talk to the boring old men over there?"

Pierre giggled then nodded as Marcus stood. He headed toward the group of town elders, Simon and the others following.

"Three men on horseback, wearing our colors, must have stood out in a town such as this."

Marcus glanced at Simon, keeping his voice low. "Agreed. Unfortunately, we're Templars on horseback. Someone is liable to accuse us of these murders."

David's eyes bulged. "You don't think—"

"I don't know what to think. This entire situation is unbelievable, yet here we are. Farmers in France, with a growing brood to care for, trying to solve the puzzle presented us. I feel like some sort of lawman nursemaid rather than a soldier serving God."

"Perhaps we should get you a nice dress."

Marcus jabbed a finger at his sergeant, though it was accompanied by a smile. "You'll be the one in the dress, if either of us is."

"I've been told I have nice legs."

"Then you shall have a pretty garland to go with it."

Simon held up his left hand daintily. "You better put a ring on it."

Marcus tossed his head back and laughed, immediately regretting it as everyone turned to see who could be so merry in such circumstances. He bowed slightly, apologizing. He approached Archambault. "I've discussed it with the boy, and he seems eager to join me on my farm until relatives can be found to care for him."

Archambault placed a hand on his chest. "Thank the good Lord. I feared the boy might not want to go, considering who he named as his parents' murderers."

"Yes, but he seems comfortable with me, and taken with the dog. I think he senses, as I, that all is not what it seems here."

"What do you mean?"

"Well, if it were indeed others from my Order who committed such a crime, would they ride here on horseback, at least three strong, wearing the colors of the Order, murder two people in cold blood, then ride out in broad daylight?" He shook his head. "Never could I believe such a thing is possible."

"Because Templars don't commit murder?" asked a man whom Marcus didn't recognize, and whose tone dripped with condescension.

"No, because Templars aren't stupid. If I were to commit this murder, I would do so disguised as a common man, who could blend in. I would not wear the uniform of my Order, unless I were begging to be caught."

"Perhaps he was. Perhaps he's a madman."

"You're forgetting something. We know there were at least three men."

"How can you be so certain?" asked Archambault.

"The boy saw two, and heard a third outside. A lookout."

"Can the boy be believed?"

Marcus shrugged slightly. "His story seems credible, and for him to have the courage to accuse Templars, when faced with four members of the Order, I think he can be taken at his word. He saw men, either genuine Templars, or men disguised as Templars, murder his parents. They were apparently looking for a document which Mr. Fabron refused to provide, then left when the lookout warned of someone coming."

"So the document may yet be inside?"

Marcus nodded. "Perhaps. I suggest you search the home for anything that might be of importance, while I attend to some business. I'll return in short order, and you can tell me what you found." Marcus turned for his horse when he paused. "And ask any of the townsfolk whether they saw a group of three or more riders this morning. They would have been traveling quickly, I'm sure."

Archambault bowed slightly. "I shall do so at once."

Outside Crécy-la-Chapelle, Kingdom of France

Second-in-command Sir Bernard had come to a decision, a decision that could be the greatest he had ever made, solidifying his future, or the worst, condemning him to a life of destitution. The latter was unlikely, as his family was wealthy, though wealth wasn't everything.

Power was.

And the respect power brought with it.

He had never been respected. Yes, his servants showed him the respect he was due growing up, but that had nothing to do with him, and everything to do with his status.

He wanted true respect. *Earned* respect.

He had been rather awkward in his youth. A fidgeter and a chronic stumbler, he couldn't put one foot in front of the other without making a spectacle of himself. He had eventually outgrown these embarrassing traits, though it had so damaged his confidence, he had never truly recovered.

And a lack of confidence meant no woman would give him the time of day.

Among the aristocracy, there were plenty of potential mates, but no matter how well off and important his family was, none of that mattered when it came to a young woman sacrificing her future happiness with someone she felt might embarrass her at every turn.

Women wanted confidence.

They wanted a man who was respected, and at a

71

minimum respected himself.

And he failed on both accounts.

But now was his chance.

Whoever could deliver the document his king was after, would be richly rewarded. And he didn't want money. He wanted the public thanks of the King, and a title granted to him because of his deeds, not his father's name.

He spotted the squire he knew possessed the document they had recovered several days ago, minutes of the meeting held by the traitors. "A word with you."

"Yes, sir."

"Has the document been transcribed yet?"

"Yes, sir. Three copies. Two have been sent to Paris already, and I retain one."

"And the original?"

"Sir Valentin felt it should remain with us."

"I will need to see it."

"Sir?"

Bernard drew a deep breath, making himself as menacing as he possibly could, something he had never done before. "You dare question me?"

It had the desired effect.

"Of course not, sir! One moment!" The squire scurried off, returning a few moments later with the document, the Templar wax seal broken by Valentin, Bernard was sure, moments after his first victim had turned it over. He unfolded it, ignoring the text, and instead focusing on the signatures at the bottom.

"Good. Off with you."

"Sir?"

Bernard gave him a look, raising the back of his hand, and the squire bolted. Bernard carefully placed the document in his saddlebags, before mounting his horse.

"Where are you going, sir?" asked his squire. "Should I accompany you?"

Bernard shook his head. "No. I have business in Paris that I must attend to. I shall return tomorrow."

"Yes, sir."

Bernard left the encampment, his shoulders square, and as determined a look as he could muster with his slamming heart. Out of the corner of his eye, Valentin glanced in his direction. Bernard urged his horse a little faster, and was soon in the trees, any calls at his back believably unheard.

And as he continued, unpursued, he breathed a little easier, realizing that should he succeed, his life would be forever changed.

Or forfeit.

St-Martin Church
Crécy-la-Chapelle, Kingdom of France

Sir Marcus stepped into the sunlight and drew a deep breath, exhaling loudly, his mood dramatically improved. There was nothing like prayer and confession to make a man feel closer to God. His difficulty fulfilling both obligations over the past few months had affected him more than he realized.

But now his conscience was clear, his penance assigned, leaving him free to focus on these unexpected events. Simon handed him the reins of his horse.

"Feeling better?"

"Much. You?"

"Like a new man with old bones."

Marcus chuckled. "I'd pray for the bones of a younger man, but I think the good Lord has more important things to listen to than the wishful thinking of an old warrior."

"This is true."

Marcus smiled down at Pierre. "And you, my young man, did you pray for your parents?"

Pierre nodded.

"And do you feel better now?"

He shrugged.

Marcus smiled at him. "No, I suppose not. But in time, you will. We will grieve together, you and I. You for your parents, and I for my sister."

"What happened to your sister?"

"She died from consumption some months ago."

Gloom threatened to cloud the boy's face, and Marcus acted quickly.

"Come, let's go to the farm. Jacques and Angeline will be there. And hopefully Mrs. Leblanc."

Marcus mounted his horse, as did the others, then reached down and swung Pierre up to rest behind him. The young boy grabbed onto him, and they all departed for the short ride to the farm on the outskirts of the village, Tanya racing ahead then stopping and staring at them before rushing back, repeating the process the entire way.

They rode mostly in silence, Marcus not wanting to discuss their situation in front of the boy, instead taking the time to think. He was convinced Templars hadn't committed this crime, but his only evidence implicated them. No one would merely take his word, so he had to prove it wasn't someone from his Order, and the only way he could think of to do that, would be to find the actual murderers.

Which meant tracking them, something he had done on innumerous occasions, though usually a Saracen in the desert, not a Christian on horseback in the green of France.

Three men disguised as Templars, on horseback and in a hurry, should have been spotted by someone. If they had been, he would at least have a direction to start in, but it was a big kingdom, and soldiers on horseback were plentiful. He couldn't imagine they kept the Templar surcoats on for long if they were imposters—they ran the risk of encountering genuine Templars who would likely recognize them for what they were.

And what were they looking for? What document could be so important that murder was the price for not handing it over? And did the auditor actually possess it? The boy had said they had asked if any other documents were signed at a meeting. They hadn't actually asked if Fabron had the document. If the boy's recollection was correct, then it was an odd question to ask. If the document did exist, and Fabron possessed it, then hopefully Archambault would have found it by the time they returned.

And would there be other victims? Were there already other victims? Did these men think only the auditor could possess the document, or was he only one of perhaps many who might?

If more were murdered by these imposters, irreparable harm could come to the good name of the Templars.

We have no time to waste.

He urged his horse on a little quicker, and they were soon on their humble farm. He handed the boy down to Simon, then dismounted. "Take a few moments to refresh yourselves, then prepare for a long ride. I fear we'll be away for at least a couple of days. If necessary, we'll resupply at one of our outposts."

Simon nodded toward the front door of the house. "Who's that beautiful thing?"

Marcus turned to see a young woman and gasped, nearly mistaking her for Nicoline, this one older than his young sister when he had last seen her twenty years ago, but much as he would have expected her to appear.

"Are you Sir Marcus?"

76

He bowed. "I am. And whom do I have the pleasure of addressing?"

"I am Isabelle Leblanc. You know my mother. She asked me to watch the children, as she had errands to run." She looked at Pierre. "And who's this?"

"Pierre. He'll be staying with us for a while."

Hands were firmly planted on hips. "Really, now? And where are his parents?"

"Dead."

Isabelle's jaw dropped, and she rushed forward as Pierre's head drooped and his shoulders shook. "You poor dear!" She embraced the boy and led him inside, glancing over her shoulder and shooting a glare at Marcus. "You could have warned me."

"Mistress, you barely gave me a chance to introduce myself."

"Next time send one of these behemoths ahead."

Marcus smiled slightly. "I yield to your superior wisdom, Mistress."

Sounds of the children inside greeted Isabelle and Pierre, and Tanya looked up at Marcus. He pointed toward the door, and she bolted to join the fun.

"Just wait until you tell her you need her to watch the children for a few days."

Marcus glanced at Simon. "Maybe I should have you tell her?"

"Are you insane? I think I just met my future wife."

Marcus nodded toward David and Jeremy, their eyes firmly planted on the doorway where Isabelle could still be seen as she busied herself with the new arrival. "I think you might have competition."

"May the best man win." Simon grinned. "Though I think she might have eyes for you."

Marcus' eyebrows shot up his forehead. "Did you raid the sacramental wine at the church? What would ever make you think such a thing?"

"Did you see the hatred in her eyes? I've only ever seen a woman look at a man that way if she was interested in him."

"She's known me for mere moments."

"You forget, she would have had months, perhaps years, of your sister talking of you, then her mother speaking of your arrival. She's built you up in her mind. The dashing knight, here to rescue her from her dreary existence in a drearier town."

"The next time you're asleep, I'm going to drill a hole in your head. I think something is wrong with that brain of yours."

David and Jeremy snickered.

"And besides, I have just reaffirmed my vows. Bedding a woman is not in my future."

Simon shrugged. "You've proven yourself to be quite the ladies' man when filled with liquor."

Marcus paused, giving Simon the eye. "I think we need to talk about your version of what happened that night, and the truth."

Simon grinned. "I'll prepare the horses."

"Uh huh, I thought you might." Marcus stepped into the house as the others headed for the barn. He regarded Isabelle for a moment, unnoticed, feeling a stirring not unfamiliar, yet always ignored. Feeling temptation wasn't the sin, it was giving in to it, and he never had.

"Go play, children, I need to talk to your uncle."

The children disappeared into the back of the house, and Isabelle turned to him. "What happened to his parents?"

"Murdered this morning, in their home."

Isabelle's hand darted to her mouth. "Oh my! Did he—?"

"Yes, he saw it."

"Who?"

"He claims it was Templars, though I suspect imposters."

She stared at his surcoat and its red cross. "Are you certain?"

He shook his head. "Without actually apprehending the men responsible, there's no way to know."

"And will you?"

"I've been asked to help."

"And you've agreed?"

"Of course. It's my duty."

She took a step closer. "And what will you do with these men should you find them?"

"I'll deliver them to the authorities so they can be tried for their crimes."

"And should they not wish to be taken?"

"They won't be given a choice."

"Will you kill them if necessary?"

"If necessary."

She appeared slightly flushed, and he found the room warmer than he should. "I suppose you'll need someone to watch the children."

He nodded. "I'm afraid so. I was hoping to find your mother so I could ask if she wouldn't mind."

"Oh, she'll mind, but"—she looked away—"I won't." She quickly returned her gaze to him. "It will, of course, be a huge imposition. I do have my own chores to tend to, but someone must look after these children when you are away." She stared at her feet. "Do you expect to be away often? I mean, in the future?"

"I'm not sure. I hope to be a farmer, and a good uncle to these children, though I am still a knight, and a Templar. I do have duties, though I have been excused from most of them."

"You'll remain a Templar?"

He bowed slightly. "Of course. It is my calling. My duty to my Lord."

She frowned. "That's unfortunate."

He stared at her, puzzled. "Why?"

"Oh, nothing." She batted a hand at him, turning toward the inner door. "I'll take care of the children while you are away. Just hurry back, for as I said, it is an imposition. A *huge* imposition."

He bowed at her back. "Of course."

Tanya appeared, sniffing at Isabelle.

"And take this creature with you. She's always underfoot!"

"Yes, Mistress." Marcus beckoned Tanya to come, the beast obeying immediately, and retreated to his bedchamber. He quickly packed what he would need, then joined the others outside, Tanya never leaving his side. He was about to mount his horse when Simon stopped him.

"Have you said goodbye to the children?"

Marcus' eyebrows shot up. "No. Why? Do you think I should?"

80

"You're their father now, for all intents and purposes. You probably should, since we might be gone awhile."

Marcus frowned then nodded. "You're right, of course." He eyed Simon. "Do *you* want to be the uncle?"

Simon grinned. "I'd rather be the husband to that gorgeous thing you've got tending to your every whim."

Marcus grunted. "Hardly. I'm quite certain she hates me."

Simon exchanged glances with the others, smiles on display.

"Are we still on that?"

"Yup. I think you have a way with the ladies that none of us were aware of."

"Now I *know* you're drunk."

Marcus reentered the home and headed for the rear where he heard the children playing. "Children!"

Tiny feet pounded the wood floor, all three appearing moments later, Isabelle following. He dropped to a knee as he imagined he should, his memories of his own father distant and faint. "I'll be leaving for a short while, perhaps a few days." Pouts appeared. "But I don't want you to worry. Mistress Leblanc here has agreed to watch over you, and I will be back before you know it. All right?"

Jacques and Angeline thrust themselves into his arms, Pierre following after a few moments of uncertainty. Marcus looked up at Isabelle helplessly as the children cried, and caught her smiling at him, the smile quickly wiped away when she spotted his eyes on her.

She stepped forward. "That's enough, children, let your uncle go."

The boys broke away, but little Angeline refused to let go, Isabelle pulling her away as Marcus' chest ached with the emotions displayed. He could only recall feeling such things when a comrade died a slow, agonizing death, an experience that had happened too many times over the years.

Though never for a child he barely knew.

For children he barely knew.

He stood, bowing slightly to Isabelle. "Thank you once again for tending to the children. I will send word if we will be away longer than expected."

"As you should."

He bowed again then beat a hasty retreat before the young woman's barbs directed at him provoked a response from the children, Pierre giving her the eye on her last remark. The boy was already showing a loyalty toward Marcus that he was surprised at, though perhaps it made sense. If Pierre had doubts that Templars were responsible, then a knight, a Templar Knight, would be the ideal protector in a young man's mind.

He hoped he could prove to him that his faith wasn't misplaced.

He stepped outside and mounted his horse, urging it forward without saying anything, still moved by the emotional display from the children.

Simon rode up beside him. "Are you all right?"

He nodded. "Yes. Just thinking."

"Uh huh."

Simon didn't sound convinced. His sergeant knew him too well, as did his squires, who wisely remained silent behind them. And as they headed back into town, he began to doubt whether he was guardian material.

Fabron Residence
Crécy-la-Chapelle, Kingdom of France

"Did you find anything?"

Bailiff's Delegate Archambault shook his head as Sir Marcus dismounted, handing the reins to David. "Nothing beyond the normal records you would expect an auditor to possess. Certainly nothing worth killing over, and nothing that wouldn't eventually be of public record." He threw his hands up in frustration. "I can find no reason for these good people to have been murdered in such a heinous fashion."

Marcus sighed. "And your people. Did they see anything?"

He nodded. "Several reported seeing three men—three Templars—on horseback, leaving toward the east shortly before the bodies were discovered."

Marcus frowned, then headed into the house to conduct his own search, disappointed in the news. He had hoped if Fabron did possess the document, then it might still be here, since his murderers had been forced to flee before they could conduct a search. But if the document weren't in the house, then either Fabron had never possessed it, or had already passed it on.

But if he had, then to whom?

And what would have been worth dying for, especially with a wife and child at risk?

It made no sense. The man was an auditor for the King, not a knight, not a soldier. He might be loyal to his king, though Marcus imagined few in this man's line of work would be loyal enough to sacrifice his family and himself for the man.

Either this document was incredibly important, or he never expected they would kill for it.

And the fact they did, suggested it was of extreme importance, and Fabron should have known so.

It simply made no sense.

What if there were no document?

His eyes widened at the thought, and he halted his search for a moment. Pierre's recollection was of the men asking *if* any other documents had been signed. If the document didn't exist, or if Fabron knew nothing of it, then that might explain his refusal to cooperate. Though they only had a scared young boy's word on what had happened, and his memory, or understanding of events, couldn't be relied upon. But if Fabron had no clue what they were talking about, he might not have realized the seriousness of the situation, and not understood that his family was at risk.

And he would never think that Templars would do such a thing.

He growled.

Tanya stared up at him.

Simon entered the room. "There's nothing here that I can see. Perhaps if we tore the place apart, we might find something, but Mr. Archambault nearly fainted when I suggested it."

Marcus grunted. "It's the King's property for use by his officials as needed. I wouldn't want to give the order either." He marched for the door. "This is a waste of time." Stepping into the slowly fading sunlight, he made to join Archambault and several elders, when he spotted a horse approaching, the rider bearing a Templar surcoat.

"It's Sir Raimond."

Marcus nodded at Simon's observation. "I wonder what he's doing here."

"He probably heard that Templars have been accused of murder."

"You might be right." He headed toward the Templar commander, holding his horse steady as the elderly man dismounted.

"Is it true?"

Marcus nodded. "The fact the accusation exists, is true. Whether or not it is accurate, is the question."

Raimond shook his head, stifling a curse. "I can't believe it could be." He shook his head emphatically. "I refuse to believe it." He lowered his voice, Marcus and Simon leaning in. "Mr. Fabron was a friend to the Templars. A trusted friend. With our Order the bank for the kingdom, we dealt with him all the time. He was always fair and just, and rarely caused any fuss like some of the others trying to curry favor with the King. And there is something else you need to know."

Marcus' eyes narrowed. "What?"

"He was at the meeting with our missing delegation."

Marcus drew a slow, deep breath as he folded his arms and tapped his chin. "Perhaps the document they were looking for came from this meeting."

Raimond stared at him. "What document?"

"According to the son, the men had a document that his father was angry they possessed. They asked if any others had been signed at a meeting. This meeting must be the one with our brothers. Mr. Fabron refused to cooperate, and that's when they killed him." He jerked a thumb over his shoulder at the house. "It's been searched twice, and no document of interest has been found."

Raimond stroked his long gray beard. "A record of the meeting would have been kept, of course, but I can't see Mr. Fabron possessing a copy of it. And even if he did, I can't see why anyone would kill over what could be in it."

Marcus agreed. "If the boy is correct, then their question suggests that the document they possessed was from that meeting, and they were looking for another. That would suggest that this document either referred to another, or contained nothing of interest to them, therefore didn't fulfill their requirements, whatever they were."

Simon cleared his throat. "What if something was discussed that was, shall we say, untoward?"

Raimond's head slowly bobbed. "Unlikely, yet anything is possible. What might be innocent to one man, could be condemning to another. We need to find the missing delegation, and find out what document these murderers might be after."

"And how do you propose we do that?" asked Marcus.

"Continue with what we discussed earlier. Go to Crèvecœur-en-Brie and meet with Sir Gilbert de St. Leger. I know he was at the meeting. That is as good a starting point as any."

Marcus nodded, then lowered his voice. "And if we should find it was Templars that committed this atrocity?"

"Then deliver them to justice if possible, kill them if necessary. Whoever is responsible for this crime must pay." He leaned in closer. "And let us all pray to the good Lord, that the boy is mistaken."

Outside Crèvecœur-en-Brie, Kingdom of France

"You know, if you're all going to be living on the farm with me, we'll have to build you proper quarters."

Simon glanced at Sir Marcus. "No need. I enjoy sleeping with animals." He grinned at David and Jeremy behind them. "And the pigs aren't bad, either."

"Haha," replied David. "If you're going to build us quarters, please give us separate rooms. The sergeant farts in his sleep."

"That was the cow."

"No, even the cow had her nose buried in the dirt trying to seek respite."

Marcus chuckled. "When we return, we'll start planning something. If we are to be farmers, then we are to be equals, at least among ourselves."

Simon grunted. "*You* will always be nobility."

"From the poorest of the poor, as you well know. I am no more noble than you are, my friend. Just because some ancestor long ago happened to wed the right person, I should be more privileged than you three?" Marcus shook his head. "I've never believed in that."

"Fortunately, you can hold those beliefs within the Order. But out here, in the real world, there is no escaping your nobility."

Marcus frowned. "Perhaps."

"And should someone object to one of us treating a noble as an equal, it may mean our heads."

Marcus glanced back at his squires. "Perhaps." He

sighed. "Very well, you may all kiss my royal ass while off the farm, but when on it, we are brothers. Agreed?"

A round of agreement and laughter responded, the men in good spirits. They had started their journey late yesterday, delayed by the unexpected events, forcing them to make camp overnight. It had been an enjoyable evening of shared stories and remembrances, and good-natured ribbing.

It was a reminder of the life he loved, and was now putting behind him.

Though not completely behind.

With his men remaining with him, there was no need for those times to end, though the battles and camaraderie of the larger contingent in the Holy Land would no longer be part of their future.

Not necessarily a bad thing.

Though he relished serving his Lord, he did not take pleasure in the killing. Yes, the Muslims were heathen infidels who deserved their fate, but he had always felt it was up to God to mete out their punishment, not man. The job of soldiers like him was to protect those on holy pilgrimages and the sacred grounds trodden by the faithful, from those who would do them harm.

If the Muslims merely kept to themselves, there would be no problem. In Jerusalem, for many years, they peacefully coexisted, until Muslims slaughtered over three thousand Christians, forcing the First Crusade. That was long before his time, and the Ninth Crusade had already come and gone, but it had all started with Muslims committing atrocities, not Christians.

And part of him was happy now to be surrounded by nothing but Christians. For the first time since he could remember, he felt perfectly at ease.

They emerged from the forest and rounded a bend leading into Crèvecœur-en-Brie. They were greeted with momentary stares, then ignored by the townsfolk, this town a metropolis compared to the tiny village of Crécy-la-Chapelle, therefore presumably more accustomed to seeing Templars.

As they should, since the Order did have a permanent presence here. Marcus was about to ask for directions when Simon pointed. "There it is."

And there it was. A large, solid stone structure with Templar flags on either side of the wide, double-doors. Sir Marcus dismounted, handing his reins to David, looking about the street for anything untoward. The building was located near the center of the town, a good number of people afoot as they went about their daily business, the riffraff keeping their distance, rather than begging for a donation to better their meager existence.

Everyone knew a Templar carried little currency on his person, due to a vow of poverty.

Which was rather ironic, considering the Order was the biggest bank in Christendom, handling most transfers of money between kingdoms and kings. Their wealth was vast, rivaling the regal customers they served, yet those who ran it were poor, paupers by any comparison.

He motioned for Simon to accompany him, and his sergeant shoved the doors open, stepping aside as he did so, bowing slightly and presenting what lay beyond with an extended arm.

"What do you think you're doing?" muttered Marcus.

"Kissing your royal ass, sir."

Marcus stifled a chuckle, stepping through the doorway, a clerk of some sort leaping to his feet at the knight now in his presence.

"Sir, my name is Xavier. How may I be of service to you?"

"I'm looking for Sir Gilbert de St. Leger. I must speak with him at once."

"I-I'm sorry, sir, but he isn't in yet. If you would like, you could wait for him here, and I will have him sent for."

The hair on the back of Marcus' neck rose. "Is it normal for him not to be in at this time?"

The young man flushed. "Umm, no sir. Quite unusual."

Marcus exchanged a concerned look with Simon, who he could tell was thinking the same thing he was.

Sir Gilbert is dead.

"You must take me to his residence at once."

Xavier hesitated.

"At once!"

"Yes, sir!" Xavier jumped several hands into the air before rushing from around his desk and toward the door. "Follow me, the barracks aren't far."

Marcus and Simon followed the young man, signaling for the squires to bring the horses, Xavier scurrying through an alleyway beside the outpost, then down a narrow street. Another building, smaller and more humble in stature, was presented by the young man, this one adorned with a single flag of the Order.

"Sir, this is where our members stay while here."

"Show us to your master's quarters."

"Yes, sir." He opened the front door and stepped inside, Marcus and Simon following. A long corridor stretched the length of the building, doors on either side, some open, revealing a kitchen, common area, and chambers with beds stacked on opposite walls. At the end of the hall, there was a single door with a plain handle. Xavier bowed slightly to Marcus. "This is it."

Marcus stepped forward, the young man clearly terrified at the prospect of disturbing his master. He rapped three times on the door, the sound echoing through the narrow hall.

Nothing.

He repeated the knock, harder this time. "Sir Gilbert de St. Leger, this is Sir Marcus de Rancourt. I must speak with you."

Again, nothing.

"Perhaps he isn't here?" suggested Xavier, false hope in his voice.

"Perhaps." Marcus opened the door and stepped inside, his heart sinking at once with the sight. A man he presumed to be Gilbert, sat on his bed, his arms out to his side, his shoulders and head resting against the stone wall, his mouth agape and eyes wide with the final moments of horror that were the end of his life.

A life ended with what appeared to be a single stab wound to the heart.

"Oh my!" cried Xavier, who swooned before collapsing. Simon reached out a hand and caught him by the belt before he slammed onto the floor. He lowered him gently to the cold stone.

Marcus' eyes swept the room. It was sparse, as to

be expected for a knight of the Order. A bed, a nightstand, a desk and chair, with a small wardrobe in the corner, the doors open, revealing the limited possessions of a man sworn to a life of poverty. A candle had burned on the nightstand, the wax now spent, probably left to burn all night. On the desk were several pieces of paper, a seal, along with another candle and a pen with ink.

And nothing more.

And nothing less.

Exactly as he would expect for a knight of the Order.

Yet this room had clearly been searched. The papers on the desk were in disarray, the lone drawer opened, and the wardrobe doors ajar. The clothes inside had been shoved apart, and the boots tossed aside.

No self-respecting knight would leave his quarters in such a state before retiring for the night.

"If there were something to find, it's been found."

Simon grunted. "Agreed. That document again?"

Marcus shrugged. "One would assume. Obviously, they didn't find it at Mr. Fabron's residence, though we were quite confident they hadn't." He stepped closer to the body, gently patting the man down to make certain his cold corpse concealed nothing.

Xavier moaned, and Simon gave him a gentle kick. "You all right, lad?"

Xavier stared up at him then thrust to his feet, staring at his master, his eyes wide. "Is he—?"

Marcus glanced at him. "Dead? Yes."

"Who-who could have done such a thing?"

"Presumably the same men who killed Mr. Fabron

and his wife in Crécy-la-Chapelle yesterday."

Xavier gasped. "Who? How?" He stopped. "How do you know of this?"

"We just came from there. It is one of the reasons we came to see your master."

"But who could do such a thing?"

"Three men dressed as Templar Knights, if the lone witness is to be believed."

Xavier gasped, his hand slapping against his open mouth. "You don't…"

"No, we don't. We believe the men to be imposters. We believe they are looking for a document that may have been written at a meeting your master recently attended."

Xavier's eyes widened. "What document?"

"We don't know. We were hoping Sir Gilbert could tell us that."

Xavier stared at the body, visibly shaking. "I-I know of only one document that my master returned from that meeting with. Merely a record of what was discussed."

Marcus inhaled with excitement. "Do you have it?"

"Locked away in his office."

"We must see it. More lives could be at stake."

Xavier appeared torn as his eyes flitted between his master, and the imposing figures of Marcus and Simon. Marcus decided to let the young man figure out his duty on his own, though his patience would last only so long.

Xavier nodded. "Very well."

He bolted from the room, and Marcus turned to follow. He glanced over his shoulder at Simon.

"Remain here. Question everyone. See if they heard or saw anything. Someone must know something."

Simon fell back and rapped hard on the first door as Marcus picked up his pace, Xavier already out the front door.

Was I ever that young?

He grunted.

Younger. But never so anxious.

Xavier didn't appear to have the temperament for battle, though sometimes when put to the test, a man could surprise even himself.

Marcus sighed.

Please Lord, let us find something that can put a stop to this insanity!

Outskirts of Paris, Kingdom of France

It had been a forbidden friendship. Or at least an accidental one. Sir Bernard had met Thomas Durant when he was a boy, when he had accompanied his father to a strange part of the city to do business with a man with a crooked nose and a hunched back.

It was an exciting journey.

He had never known such parts of Paris existed. The squalor and filth were something to behold for a young boy raised among the elite, and while they rode in their ornate carriage, he had reveled in the awe shown by those his age.

It had been a rush, a rush he wished he could feel once again.

Yet today, riding through these streets, nobody showed him any respect beyond getting out of his way. He was just another knight on horseback, to be ignored lest he ask something of them. Even the children kept their distance rather than chance asking for a spare coin or two.

And though on any other day he'd have actually missed the attention, today he was grateful he wasn't receiving it. For the man he wanted to meet, was not a good man, though a necessary one, and if he was good enough for his father to do business with, then he was good enough for him.

He hadn't seen Thomas in years, and in fact, had only seen him perhaps a couple of dozen times in their youth, and then only when one of them sneaked away. Boys of his station weren't supposed to associate with the great unwashed, yet he had the most exciting conversations with Thomas, some of the best he had ever had.

But in time, as most things from childhood had a habit of doing, the relationship grew more distant, and eventually ended, as the realities of manhood thrust them apart, the innocence of youth's ignorance no longer permitted.

Yet to this day, he still missed Thomas, and a surge of excitement gripped him as he spotted their humble home, a shingle out front indicating the proprietor inside offered reading and writing services.

What it didn't mention was his side business.

He dismounted in front of the residence, and a young boy rushed forward to tend to his horse. He dropped a coin in the boy's hand, and a grin revealed rotting teeth.

"Make sure she is watered and fed, and brush her down good. There'll be another of those for you if I'm satisfied."

"Yes, milord!"

Bernard opened the door to the small shop on the main floor of the residence, blinking as his eyes adjusted to the dim interior. Someone in the shadows rose, chair legs scraping on wood revealing their position.

"Ah, may I help you, sir?"

Bernard closed the door behind him and stepped forward. "Are you Mr. Durant?"

The man bowed. "At your service, sir."

"I am Sir Bernard de Claret. Perhaps you remember my father. You performed a service for him in the past."

The man bowed even deeper. "Of course! Of course! How is your father? He is well, I trust?"

"He is, thank you. And your good wife?"

The old man sighed. "I'm afraid we lost her some years ago."

Bernard frowned. "You have my sympathies. And your son? Thomas?"

Durant wagged a finger at him. "Ahh, your old friend, correct? I knew of your secret. Foolish boy, he was. You broke his heart, you know."

Bernard's chest ached, and his throat went dry. "It is one of my greatest regrets."

"But unavoidable, I'm sure. Nobility does not mix with the peasantry."

Bernard remained silent.

"But you asked of him, and I failed to respond. He is well. In fact, he should be here any moment. Why don't we discuss your business before he returns?" Durant gestured toward a chair, and Bernard took it, the old man returning to his perch behind his desk, a desk covered in documents and letters. "What is it you need from me?"

"What I am about to ask of you must never be discussed with anyone, understood?"

"Oh, of course. Discretion is extremely important in my business."

"Should it be discovered that what you produce is not, shall we say, genuine, it could bring embarrassment to the King himself."

Durant's eyes bulged.

"You understand what that could mean?"

Durant's head bobbed rapidly. "I do."

"And you wish to proceed?"

"I-I'm not sure—"

Bernard tossed a purse filled with coins on the desk, the thud indicating a generous offering.

"—if I could possibly say anything to the contrary." The purse was quickly grabbed and emptied into a shaking left hand, counted with a steady right. "You, sir, are either very generous, or very, umm, motivated?"

Bernard smiled. "I see we understand each other." He produced the document, handing it over to the old man. "I need a document created, the text of which we will create together, as I suspect you may have a more devious mind than I, but the signatures at the bottom of this one must be transcribed exactly onto the new document. There can be no margin for error. The men whose signatures these belong to must themselves believe they actually signed the document we are to create. Are you up to the task?"

The old man examined the document with a magnifying glass, leaning in closer to read the signatures, his eyes flaring as he no doubt recognized some of the names. He put the magnifying glass down, then looked up at Bernard with a smile. "Absolutely, but I have one question."

Bernard frowned. "What is it?"

"Whom is this for?"

Bernard debated giving the man an answer, then decided if he should, it should be one that elicited the desired response. "The King himself."

Durant sucked in a quick breath and nodded. "Then we shall begin at once."

Templar Barracks
Crèvecœur-en-Brie, Kingdom of France

Simon rapped on the next door, having learned nothing of value so far. Few who had spent the night were still there, and those who were, remembered nothing. From all accounts, it was an uneventful evening, with most retiring early for their journeys or duties the next day.

And this room appeared empty as well.

He opened the door and confirmed it.

He sighed.

"Are you looking for someone in particular?"

Simon turned to find a short, large woman, mixing a bowl of something. "No, but I am looking for information."

She laughed. "Information! What kind of information could you possibly find here?" She stepped back out of sight, and Simon followed her into what turned out to be a kitchen, preparations for lunch already underway.

"Were you here last night?"

She nodded. "Until the last of your brothers retired for the night, then I left for home. I barely got to see my husband. If he doesn't get his attentions then he gets cranky!" She roared with laughter, tossing the bowl onto the table occupying the center of the room.

Simon smiled slightly, the woman no doubt a handful in the bedchambers. "Did you see any strangers?"

She picked up a knife and paused, giving him a look. "You are aware of what this place is, aren't you? Strangers are our business. We have men coming and going constantly. Only those stationed in the town stay here more than a night or two."

Simon frowned. "Did anyone visit Sir Gilbert?"

She paused before attacking several carrots with the blade. "Yes, now that you mention it. Two men arrived, just before I was about to leave, asking to see him. I showed them to Sir Gilbert's chambers, then left for the night, as they said they weren't staying."

Simon's heart rate picked up a few beats. "Could you describe them?"

She shrugged. "Two men, about your height, one with a beard, the other just a mustache. That's about it."

Simon hesitated to ask, but knew he had to. "Were they, umm, Templars?"

"Of course they were. Only Templars are permitted in here."

Simon sighed. "Knights?"

She nodded. "I hardly think a sergeant or lowly squire would impose upon Sir Gilbert at that time of night."

"Did you hear any of their conversation?"

"None."

"None at all? Even when they exchanged pleasantries?"

She paused, knife in mid-slice. "Yes, I suppose I did, though I quickly closed the door. I heard little beyond 'good day.'"

"Did you hear any names?"

She shook her head. "No, I'm sorry."

"Were they friendly?"

"Quite. Gentlemanly, as I should expect from the Order, though one seemed a little uncertain of himself."

Simon's eyes narrowed. "What do you mean?"

"He just didn't have the bearing of a knight, as I've come to expect. You lot are usually quite confident. This one seemed…"

"Nervous?"

She shook her head. "No, I wouldn't call it that." She snapped her fingers. "Deferential! He rarely spoke, and he never looked anyone in the eye, as if he were inferior to his companion."

Simon grunted. "Doesn't sound like any Templar Knight I've ever met."

"So, why all the questions?"

Simon frowned, this woman obviously not yet having heard the sad news. "Your master is dead. Murdered in the night, quite possibly by the very men you described."

The knife dropped onto the cutting board, the woman onto the floor.

Durant Residence
Paris, Kingdom of France

Sir Bernard reread the proposed document, and a shiver rushed up and down his spine. It was good. It was devious. It was everything Valentin was searching for.

And now *he* had it.

Or he soon would.

The old man stared at him, worry on his face, his left hand still trembling, though he thankfully wrote with his right. "Are you sure you want me to create this?"

The fear in his voice was evident from the tremor not there earlier, and the hushed tone suggested he feared the ears that passed on the other side of the dilapidated walls. Yet Bernard understood his fear. In fact, he shared it. But this was a means to an end. A way for him to be the hero, to earn his station and name on his own.

So what if the document was a forgery? Nobody beyond him and Mr. Durant would know, and this terrified old man would tell no one. He would create a forgery so perfect, no one would be able to tell, not even those purported to have written it, and *he* would be the one who found what the King had sent his best to find, and *he* would be the hero at the end of the day—*not* that disrespectful cretin Valentin.

He stared at the old man. "Absolutely."

Durant sighed. "Very well."

"How long will you need?"

"I will work through the night. The sooner this is out of my home, the better. You shall have it tomorrow morning at first light."

Bernard leaned back and smiled. "Excellent. That gives me plenty of time to get back, and this can all be finished before day's end." The front door of the shop opened, and Bernard spun toward the new arrival, his hand reaching for his sword. He stopped, a smile spreading. "Thomas!"

His boyhood friend stared at him for a moment, puzzled, no doubt still trying to recognize a voice from the past while his eyes adjusted to the dim light. "Bernard? Is that you?"

Bernard leaped to his feet, rushing toward his friend and embracing him. "Thomas! It's so good to see you! How long has it been?"

Thomas stared at him before replying, his mouth agape. "I-I'm not sure. Four years? Five?"

Bernard held him at arm's length, looking him up and down, his heart heavy with the sight of his emaciated frame and threadbare clothes. Business obviously wasn't good, though perhaps the heavy purse he had laid upon Thomas' father might buy him a new set of clothes and some good, solid food for a time. "You look good."

"And you still lie well."

Bernard tossed his head back and laughed, letting go of his friend. "Your brutal honesty is what I have missed, my friend."

"You look like you've done well for yourself." Thomas held up a bag of potatoes, showing it to his father.

"Is that payment from Mr. Rivard?"

"I'm afraid so, Father."

Durant shook his head. "No one pays in coin anymore." He held up the purse presented earlier. "Present company excluded, of course."

Bernard bowed slightly.

Thomas rushed to the table, taking the purse from his father, tossing it from one hand to the other, as if trying to guess its weight. "What is this for?"

"Some work I'm having your father do for me. Nothing you need concern yourself with."

"I, umm, must get started. Why don't you two boys go somewhere and catch up? Leave me to my work."

Bernard beamed. "A splendid idea. Let us go somewhere and get us some food and drink." He poked Thomas' ribs. "You look like you could use a good feeding."

Thomas turned away slightly, as if ashamed, leaving a pit in Bernard's stomach. Thomas motioned toward Bernard's garb. "I don't think there is any place near here that you would be satisfied with.

"Nonsense! You wouldn't believe the taverns I have frequented on my journeys throughout the kingdom. And besides, I want to spend time with you! Who knows when I'll be back in these parts?"

"Yes, who knows," murmured Thomas, Bernard getting the distinct impression his friend was uncomfortable with the prospect of spending time with him.

Is he that ashamed of his station, or does he not want to be seen with me?

He stared at his friend. "Would you prefer, perhaps, that we stay in and catch up, just the two of us?"

Thomas brightened with the suggestion, leaving Bernard relieved it wasn't that his friend didn't want to be with him, it was that he didn't want to be associated with him. Understandable. Should the locals think he had a connection to nobility, it could make things difficult for him. Bernard pulled out several coins. "How about you fetch us some food and drink, and we'll enjoy ourselves in the privacy of your home."

Thomas grinned at the sight of the coins, and Bernard hoped, the suggestion. "Splendid idea. I'll be back shortly."

He bolted from the shop, leaving Bernard once again alone with his friend's father. The old man looked up at him.

"Don't take it personally, sir. Being seen with you would present difficulties."

Bernard nodded. "I understand." He stepped back toward the table, tapping a finger on the work in progress. "And let us both ensure he never knows of our business."

Durant stared up at him, his left hand shaking once again. "Of that, you can be certain."

Templar Outpost
Crèvecœur-en-Brie, Kingdom of France

Sir Marcus sat behind the late Sir Gilbert's desk, unfolding the only known document to have been produced at the meeting between the Templar delegation sent from the Holy Land, and the Order's supporters in the region.

And it was rather disappointing.

As he scanned the document, he realized it was nothing more than a record of who was in attendance, routine matters that couldn't be considered scandalous by anyone, even the most paranoid, then the signatures of those there to witness the document. And the numerals indicating it was the fifth of six copies.

He quickly recorded the names, noting Fabron and Sir Gilbert were among them, then handed the list to young Xavier. "I'll need the whereabouts of these men."

Xavier stared at it for a moment. "I know where some *should* be, in fact most, but I can't guarantee they're still there."

"No matter. Give me what you know, then send messengers to find the others. I'll give you our planned route as best I can, so you can have word sent as you find the others."

Xavier bowed. "Yes, sir." He disappeared from the room, only to be replaced by Simon moments later, his sergeant closing the door behind him.

"Find anything?"

He nodded, taking a seat in front of the desk now occupied by Marcus. "I found a woman that works there who saw two men, dressed as Templar Knights, who asked to see Sir Gilbert."

"When?"

"Last night. Late. She was apparently about to head home to bed her husband."

Marcus blushed slightly. "Apparently this woman was a fountain of information."

"She did like to talk," chuckled Simon. "She said one had a beard, the other just a mustache, and that one of them appeared 'deferential'—her word—unlike any knight of our Order I've heard of, from the description she gave of his manner."

"Yet more evidence to suggest imposters."

Simon nodded. "Agreed."

"And did she hear anything?"

"Nothing beyond gentlemanly greetings before she closed the door."

"My guess is the same two who killed Mr. Fabron. The third was probably keeping watch outside."

"Yes. And until we find out why they're killing, we could end up simply discovering body after body, making no headway in capturing these murderers."

Marcus waved the document in front of him. "We may have something, finally."

"What is it?"

"It's the document our young clerk referred to. It's the minutes of the meeting held with the delegation from the Holy Land."

"Anything of interest?"

Marcus shook his head. "Nothing scandalous, if

that's what you mean. But it might still help us."

Simon leaned forward and took the document. "How?"

"The list of signatories at the bottom. At least two are dead already. I believe our suspected imposters have this same list, perhaps a copy of this very document, and are going from one person to the next, trying to find this other mystery document."

Simon placed the paper back on the table, his head bobbing slowly. "That makes sense. If we could figure out whom they plan to see next, we might be able to stop them."

Marcus shook his head. "They have at least half a day on us. We won't be able to save the next victim, but perhaps we could save the one after him."

"If we can determine the order they are killing them in."

Marcus nodded. "Exactly."

"But how are we going to do that?"

"I've got Xavier putting together the locations for the names on the list. I'm hoping there will be some sort of pattern shown."

Simon rose from his chair, walking over to a map on the wall showing the region. He pointed. "This is where we now call home, where we found Mr. Fabron and his wife. And this is where we are now."

Xavier entered the room, holding a piece of paper. "I was able to find all but two. I'll send a messenger immediately to the regional headquarters to find out their usual location."

"Excellent work." Marcus rose, gesturing for Xavier to join him at the map. "Now show us where these men are in relation to where we are."

The young man nodded, pulling pins from the top of the map and shoving them rapidly into ten locations, including the two they had already identified. All were northeast of their current location. Marcus smiled, pointing at the two closest. "They'll be going to one of these two locations next." He turned to Xavier. "Send two of your fastest messengers to these men immediately. Warn them of the danger."

Xavier bowed rapidly. "Yes, sir!" He disappeared, and Marcus returned his attention to the map, Simon already pointing to a lone pin farther to the northeast. "We have no way of knowing which of these two they will hit next, and I don't think splitting up is wise." He tapped the third pin. "This is where I think we should go. We should have no problem getting there before them, since they'll have two men to kill first."

Marcus sighed. "I hate having to decide this. If we go to either one of these first two men, we have an even chance of saving one."

"Yes, sir, but should we choose poorly, he will already be dead, as will the next. We will then be in a race to get to the third before these fiends."

Marcus agreed reluctantly. "But go directly to the third, and we will absolutely save him, and be able to put an end to this, once and for all."

"Exactly."

Marcus spun on his heel, heading for the door, but not before grabbing the document from the desk. "We must leave at once, and pray our messengers reach the next two targets first."

Durant Residence
Paris, Kingdom of France

Sir Bernard emptied his cup once again, and his childhood friend replenished it with wine that tasted better as the night wore on. One couldn't expect a fine vintage in these parts, and it had been painful to drink those first few cups, though now that he was feeling no pain, he didn't mind it at all.

And neither did Thomas Durant. His friend had been a little uncomfortable at first, but after the wine flowed, he became more at ease, and the conversation had been jovial since. Bernard couldn't remember the last time he had enjoyed someone's company so much. He was never comfortable around his family, a group far too proper to allow something as distasteful as fun to interrupt their dinner parties, he had few if any real friends, and his fellow soldiers treated him as if he were a joke.

Especially that cretin Valentin.

"So the life of a knight at the service of the King must be rewarding."

Bernard grunted. "You'd think so, but I haven't found it so."

Thomas pulled a chunk off the quail they had been nibbling on all evening. "What's the problem? Boredom?"

"Disrespect."

Thomas swallowed his bite, his eyes widening. "Who would dare disrespect a knight?"

"His fellow knights." He sighed. "Can I tell you

something? Man to man, as a friend?"

"Of course! You know you can tell me anything, and it shall remain in my confidence."

Bernard glanced about the empty room, Thomas' father not seen all night, and lowered his voice. "My so-called brothers treat me like a fool, as if I were a joke to them. And their disrespect, shown in front of the men I command, means they too look upon me with disdain." His chest tightened, and tears threatened to reveal themselves. "It's as if I am nothing but an object of ridicule with them. I wish sometimes I could just run away, and leave all of this behind."

Thomas refilled his cup. "Why don't you?"

Bernard laughed. "Right! And embarrass my family? I would be disowned, lose my title, and be forced to come live with you!"

Thomas grinned. "We could be roommates like we always talked about."

Bernard sighed. "What wonderfully naïve notions we had back then."

Thomas closed his eyes and leaned back. "Ahh, to be young again, when you didn't understand the responsibilities that lay ahead of you, and I didn't know what it meant to be a poor man in a rich man's world."

Bernard smiled at his friend. "Is it really that hard? Life for you, I mean?"

Thomas opened his eyes and nodded. "You have no idea, and I'm happy for you that you never will. There is little work, and what little there is, doesn't pay well and isn't reliable. Few need my father's services, and though I can read and write, I know it's his hidden talents that really pay the bills."

"Hidden talents?"

Thomas gave him a look. "You know full-well what I'm talking about. I know you are here to see him, and not me, and no one pays what you did for a few letters. You're availing yourself of his talents." He waved a hand in front of him. "Don't worry, I won't ask what for. That's between you and him, but all that to say, I don't have his talents, and reading and writing for the illiterate will not keep me in food and shelter after my father passes."

Bernard frowned, staring at his friend. The very notion that he could end up on the streets, begging, only to die from the elements, or worse, of starvation, was heart-wrenching. "Maybe I can help you."

Thomas stared at him for a moment. "I wasn't asking for charity, I was merely confiding in a friend. I don't want, nor need, your pity."

Bernard was slightly taken aback by the words, and for a moment, the hurt threatened to be replaced by anger.

Yet how were these words any different from the words he had said to himself over the years, when everything he had was given to him because of a title he hadn't earned, but instead had been born into.

He wanted to be his own man, and he could understand why Thomas would feel the same way.

He smiled. "And you don't have it, I assure you. You are a proud man, and I respect that, I truly do. You have more pride in yourself than I do in myself, I can assure you. What I meant was, when I earn my own reputation, my own station, I will need good people to work for me." He leaned closer to his friend. "Should you ever find yourself desperate, there will be no shame in coming to me and asking for a job. I will make sure you never starve, or lack for warmth. You have my word as your friend."

Thomas smiled slightly, his tensed muscles at the perceived slight, visibly relaxing. "I'm sorry, my friend. I should not have taken offense." He raised his cup. "Should you earn the station you desire, I shall not hesitate to seek you out should my situation demand it." He smiled. "But not a moment before."

Bernard laughed. "Not a moment before!" He slammed his cup against his friend's, then drained it. "And I hope soon that I will be able to fulfill my promise made this fine evening, thanks to your father."

Thomas refilled both their cups. "To your success, and my father's steady hand!"

Another drink was had, and the warmth continued to spread through Bernard's body, relaxing his tired muscles, and loosening his tight tongue. He lowered his voice. "Can you keep a secret?"

Thomas leaned closer, his elbow slipping off the table, his chin slamming into the unforgiving wood. Bernard roared with laughter, Thomas joining in.

"I'm drunk!"

"Yes, you are!" cried Bernard. "So am I!"

"Then if you are, you shouldn't be telling me secrets!"

Bernard reached across the table and slapped his friend on the arm. "If I can't trust my best friend, then whom can I trust?"

Thomas raised his cup in salute. "This is true! This is true!"

Bernard lowered his voice again. "Do you want to know my secret?"

Thomas leaned in close, his voice a harsh whisper. "Yes, of course I do. What dastardly plan have you concocted?"

Bernard grinned. "Dastardly. I like that. I've figured out a way to get everything I want, and to make those insolent cretins who would mock me, rue the day they did."

"Tell me!"

"The document your father is preparing for me will seal my fate, as it will those named in it."

Thomas paused. "What do you mean?"

"I mean, everyone named will be dead within the week, their Order destroyed, and I will be owed a great debt of gratitude by the King himself."

Thomas drew away slightly. "Who? Who are you talking about?"

Bernard sneered. "The Knights Templar, and those who would support them rather than our King."

116

Outside Coulommiers, Kingdom of France

Sebastien tossed the stick, his dog racing after it, eagerly returning a few moments later, the process repeated yet again. It was a beautiful day, and his constitutional after tending to his morning chores was always a joy, this the only moment of peace he had on any given day.

Home was chaos.

Six kids, none older than eight, and a wife with the shrillest of voices one could imagine. He loved her, no one could doubt that, but when she raised her voice at the children, birds took flight for as far as the eye could see.

He swore she could cause a migration south if she really put her mind to it.

His friends ribbed him about it, since they had known each other since they were toddlers, and she had always had a volume that caused dogs to cringe. But it didn't matter. She was perfect in every other way.

Yet he still needed his peace. Just half an hour a day. With the animals tended to, he had taken off this morning as he did every morning, his mutt eagerly accompanying him, a good guard against any brigand on the road. He had never encountered any problems before, though had heard tales from other townsfolk that would make a man's skin crawl, though he occasionally had his doubts.

Yet it was still wise to bring the dog.

He tossed the stick once again, and once again the

eager beast raced after it, then abruptly bolted to the left and into the trees.

"Parceval, get back here!"

He was ignored, and uttered a mild invective before heading into the trees after him.

"Parceval, where are you?"

He didn't have to go far to find the mutt digging at the ground in a small clearing, a clearing that appeared to have been freshly dug up. His eyes narrowed and he tensed as he glanced about, searching the trees for unwelcome guests. Somebody had been here, the footprints evidence of that, and there had been many more than one. The area dug up was large, quite large, so whatever had been left here must have been substantial. This wasn't a hastily dug grave. This was the work of men intent on hiding something significant from view.

Treasure?

The thought at once thrilled and terrified him. Treasure meant something worth protecting, and therefore worth killing for. But it could also mean a way out of the poverty-stricken existence he and his family would suffer their entire lives.

Even just a few gold coins could mean insurance against a failed crop, or an illness that might spread through the pigs.

Which was why when Parceval started tugging at something that shone, he dropped to his hands and knees to help, rather than run away.

He nearly vomited when a pale hand appeared.

"Get away!" he ordered, shoving him aside. The dog backed off, though was soon digging again, a few paces away. Sebastien tugged at the hand, revealing an arm, then began digging, a gray-bearded face revealed.

A branch snapped behind him and he spun, his heart racing, but he saw nothing.

Calm down. There's no one here.

He kept digging, and nearly shouted in triumph when he found a small purse on the man's person. He eagerly untied it with shaking hands, eventually pouring its contents into his palm.

Coins totaling four *deniers*.

Four? That's all?

Judging by what the man was wearing, he was clearly a knight, though he curiously bore no markings. He could think of no knight who would carry only four *deniers* on his person.

Perhaps those who killed him took the rest.

Then why would they leave the four? It wasn't as if it were well hidden. It made no sense to him.

Parceval barked.

He looked over to see another arm exposed. He scrambled over on his hands and knees, and began digging again, redirecting Parceval to get started a few paces away. Another distinguished beard was revealed, and another purse, again with four *deniers*.

Poor knights?

And with no surcoats to indicate whom they served?

Poor knights.

His jaw dropped as a thought occurred to him.

Parceval barked again, a hoof exposed.

Oh my!

He made the sign of the cross, then leaped to his feet, grabbing Parceval by the scruff of the neck and pulling him from the mass grave.

A mass grave that had to belong to Templar Knights.

The only Order he knew of who had taken a vow of poverty, and were limited to no more than four *deniers* on their person.

Outside Saint-Augustin, Kingdom of France

Sir Valentin stood, arms stretched out to the sides as his squire prepared him for the journey ahead. They were less than an hour's ride from their next target. They would interrogate him, eliminate him should they not find what they were looking for, and continue on to the next.

But if we do find it...

The mission would immediately change. He had arrest warrants with him already, just awaiting the names to put on them. The initial document they had recovered named names, but there was nothing incriminating. It was a useless document beyond identifying who should be questioned.

It would lead to no arrests, no convictions.

And a disappointed King.

Something he dared not risk.

"Done, sir."

He tested his range of motion, nodding with satisfaction. "Where is Sir Bernard? Has he returned yet?"

His squire shook his head. "I have not seen him, sir. And I already inquired of his squire, as I knew you would ask."

Valentin frowned. "If that fool doesn't return before dusk, I'll issue a warrant for *his* arrest!"

Several of his men within earshot glanced in his direction before returning to their duties, none wanting to risk his attention when he was angry. He didn't blame them. When he wanted to be, he could be quite friendly with his men. After all, many were knights, many equal in family name, attending the same parties and schools.

But here, in these woods, *he* was in charge. This was *his* mission.

Its success would be his.

And its failure.

He mounted his horse, using the vantage point to scan the area for the incompetent second-in-command thrust upon his handpicked group of the best.

And he had no success.

The man is a bumbling fool, and could sabotage this mission through ineptitude.

He grunted to himself.

Perhaps not *having him here would be a good thing.*

Durant Residence
Paris, Kingdom of France

The hairs on the back of Sir Bernard's neck rose as he examined the document prepared by his friend's father. It was incredible. If he didn't know it was a complete fabrication, if he weren't the one who had helped script its dastardly contents, he could be forgiven for rushing into the streets and demanding the arrest of every signatory to the treasonous document.

But he did know.

And it still thrilled him.

This one piece of paper will secure my future, and rid me of my inglorious past.

He stared at the signatures, comparing them to the original document he had stolen, trying to find any hint they were forgeries, and failing. As explained by Mr. Durant, slight variations were included so that no one could claim these were just a copy of those on the original document, but where it counted, in the swirls and spacing, everything matched just so.

No one would know.

He closed his eyes for a moment, massaging his temples as the unforgiving headache he had suffered all morning continued its assault. He had drunk far too much the night before, though from what he remembered, it had all been good fun.

He had missed Thomas, and was determined to maintain their friendship.

Did you promise to give him a job?

He strained to remember the conversation.

"So you are satisfied with the work?"

Bernard nodded, immediately regretting it. "Yes. You have outdone yourself, as I'm sure you did with my father's work so long ago." He smiled, lowering his voice. "Does my father still avail himself of your special talents?"

Durant waved his hands in front of him. "I never discuss the affairs of others, as I'm sure you wouldn't want me discussing yours."

Bernard smiled, pleased with the answer. "Of course, as you shouldn't." He rose from his chair carefully, taking care not to move his swollen head too swiftly. The old man placed the finished work in a large folded piece of thicker paper, handing it to him, along with the original document. Bernard placed both in his pouch, wishing for a moment his squire was here to tend to him.

Oh my!

The evening's conversation suddenly came rushing back. His shameful admission of his past failures, his revelations of a plan to earn his title, and then, most horrifically, the painstaking details confessed to a boyhood friend he barely knew anymore, with the promise to take care of him should anything happen to him in the future.

Thomas knew.

He knew everything.

His heart slammed, and his panic roared through his ears as his head pounded in protest. Nobody could know. Nobody. If it should ever come out what he had done, it could mean his life. It *would* mean his life. The boy he knew years ago could be trusted, but could the young, desperate, starving man he had reunited with last night? And could his father, a man struggling to survive with a failing business?

What set of circumstances would cause either one of them to decide discretion wasn't worth an empty belly?

He placed his hand casually on his dagger. "Where is your son? I would like to say goodbye to him."

Durant rose, rounding the table. "I'm afraid he's already gone. He had some work in the market. It's rare to be hired, so despite his condition, he did his duty."

"A fine son you have raised."

Durant smiled. "He's my greatest creation. Far more so than anything these hands have done."

Bernard patted the pouch. "A wonderful sentiment." He returned his hand to the dagger. "And when shall he return?"

"Not until nightfall, I'm afraid. He did ask me to tell you that he had a wonderful time, and should you ever be so inclined, he would enjoy dining and conversing again with his old friend."

Bernard's heart ached for more reason than one. He *had* enjoyed himself. More than any time he could recall in his adult life. He did want to maintain that friendship lost so long ago.

And he had to make certain there were no witnesses.

He drew his dagger, plunging it into the old man's stomach, then yanked the blade high, scrambling his innards. The old man gasped, his eyes bulging with confusion and pain as he gripped at the dagger.

"Why?" he croaked as Bernard pulled the knife

free before stepping back as his friend's father reached out with a blood-soaked hand.

"Because none can know our secret."

"Please, not my son." Durant collapsed to his knees, then fell to his side, still reaching toward Bernard. "Please, spare him."

Bernard's eyes clouded with tears as his chest burned. "I'm sorry, but he knows too much."

"Please…"

Bernard couldn't watch any longer, and instead turned on his heel and left the humble shop and home of the only true friend he had ever had, with the realization that the next time he saw Thomas, he'd be forced to kill him too.

For he must preserve the secret.

At all costs.

Templar Commandry
Coulommiers, Kingdom of France

Sir Raimond leaned back, thankful his glory days were over. He had fought too many battles to count, some with thousands of his brothers against the Saracen hordes, some alone against brigands determined to steal from the defenseless pilgrims on their way to the Holy Land.

But he hadn't spilled a drop on the soil of his home, France.

He had fully expected to die long before reaching his current age, but the good Lord had watched over him, preserving him for some reason, a reason that though he wasn't aware of, he was certain his Lord was.

And that was good enough for him.

Life was a gift, and he wasn't going to waste it, nor question why he had been left to live long past his time.

And he also wasn't going to begrudge himself a nap, whenever he felt the need.

As he did now.

His eyes drooped, the price to pay for remaining awake late into the night, worrying about Sir Marcus and his men, about the murders—now numbering three—and the whereabouts of the missing delegation from the Holy Land.

He let out a long, loud breath, his head tilting slightly to the side as blissful sleep finally overwhelmed him.

A hard rap on his door had him bolting upright in his chair, wondering how long he had been out. He frowned, the sun, visible through his window, in the same position it had been the last time his eyes had gazed upon it.

"Come in."

The door opened, and his young clerk stepped inside, bowing his apologies. "I'm sorry to disturb you, sir, but someone is demanding to see you."

Raimond sighed. "Who?"

"He says his name is Sebastien. He says he found something you must see."

Raimond closed his eyes for a moment, a frown spreading.

He wiped it off.

He didn't know what this man's business was, and the stranger at least deserved his initial respect. Whether he continued to have it, remained to be seen. "Show him in."

His clerk disappeared, returning a moment later with a humbly dressed man, his well-worn face and rough hands indications he led a hard, honest life.

"I am Sir Raimond, commander of this outpost. State your business."

"Sir Raimond, I found something that you must see."

"What is it?"

"Bodies, sir. At least two. And a horse!"

Raimond tensed as his immediate thoughts were of the missing delegation. "Where?"

"In the forest outside of town, near my farm. I was taking my morning constitutional when my dog ran

128

off. I found what looks to be some sort of grave."

"Why would you bring this information to me, and not your local officials?"

The man lowered his voice. "I fear they may be yours, sir, they may be Templars."

Raimond's heart was hammering now, but he had to be cautious. "What evidence do you have of this? Were they wearing our markings?"

The man shook his head rapidly. "No, sir, they weren't. In fact, they weren't wearing anything that could identify them."

Raimond relaxed slightly. "Then why would you think they were of the Order?"

The man held out his hand, a small purse clasped within. "Because of this."

Raimond took the purse and emptied it into his palm, gasping at what he saw.

Four *deniers*.

"Bring me my horse at once!"

Approaching the Durant Residence
Paris, Kingdom of France

Thomas Durant was both angry and disappointed. He had hoped to earn some much-needed money today working in the market, but when he had arrived, he was informed the shipment had been delayed, and he shouldn't bother returning the next day.

The anger came from spotting the shipment in an alley, a crew he knew belonged to a local gang, unloading it. If he were willing to compromise his principles, he too could have been working that load, but in exchange for half his pay.

He wasn't there yet.

But someday, he might be.

That's when you call upon Bernard.

He smiled. He had truly enjoyed himself last night, and he had never feasted or drank like that in his entire life. In fact, his head still pounded, and his full belly was still protruding more than he recalled, though he wondered if that were just his imagination.

A full belly.

What a wonderful feeling.

If Bernard were successful in his plan, there could be little doubt word would spread, and at least then he would know he had a way out of this horrible life. Though he would never leave his father. He would stay to take care of him until God finally came for him, and he prayed that was many years yet.

But he was getting old.

And he wasn't well.

The tremors were getting worse, though only affected his left hand and arm for now. The moment it spread to his right, their main source of income would disappear. And no matter how meager that income might be, it was essential to their survival.

Maybe you will have to leave him, to save him.

The very thought broke his heart. To leave and work for Bernard, sending money to his father, yet not seeing him, was a nightmare imagining.

But if it meant saving his father's life?

He sighed. Leaving the old man alone would probably kill him. The death of his mother almost had, yet his father had pushed on for his son. It tortured him daily that his father was suffering, continuing to work, just to support him.

I need to do something more!

He rounded the corner and smiled as he saw Bernard mounting his horse, though before he could call out to him, he was already galloping away, charging through the crowds as if the King himself had ordered him to ignore the safety of those he shared the road with.

I hope he succeeds, for Papa's sake.

Though part of him didn't. The bits and pieces he remembered from last night were horrifying, if recalled correctly. The document his father had created was meant to bring down the Templars. Though he had no love for them, he had nothing against them. His dealings with them had always been of indifference. They were warrior monks with vast holdings across Christendom, and he was not.

Perhaps I could join them.

His eyebrows rose at the prospect. He was already poor, so a vow of poverty would mean nothing. But chastity? Only the knights were truly sworn to that, and he could never rise to that level, yet the very thought was horrifying.

He loved women.

Though he had never been with one.

He had kissed Sophie once, in the alley behind her home, and it had been the most thrilling experience of his life, stirring things he didn't know could be.

But that was years ago.

Young women weren't interested in men with no prospects, and he had none. He could read and write, which was unusual in these parts, but that was it. If he were to open up his own shop, all he would do was put his own father out of work, there not enough business for one of them, let alone two.

He opened the front door, stepping inside. "Papa! It's me! They stole my shift again." He blinked several times then gasped at the sight before him. His father was lying on the floor, in front of his desk, a pool of blood surrounding him. "Papa!" He rushed forward and dropped to his knees, shaking his father by the shoulder. "Papa!"

His father groaned.

"Papa! Who did this?"

"Ber…"

"Bernard?"

His father grunted.

His world closed in around him at the very notion, at the very idea that his friend could have done such a thing. It was inconceivable.

Yet was it?

132

His so-called friend was plotting to destroy the Templars to curry favor with the King. He had his father create a forged document that would lead to the death of untold numbers of innocents.

Why should he be at all surprised this man, this stranger, had tried to kill his father?

"Why, father? Why did he do this?"

"Document."

"The forgery?" His jaw dropped as he realized why. "He didn't want anyone who knew it existed to live?"

His father nodded, his skin so pale and cold to the touch that Thomas knew the poor soul only had moments to live.

"I'll go get help."

His father reached out with what must have been the last of his strength, and grabbed his wrist. "No. Stay." He moaned, then opened his eyes, staring into Thomas'. "Must save yourself. He-he'll be back."

A shiver raced up his spine at the thought. His father was right. If he hadn't gone to work this morning, Bernard likely would have killed him too. The fact he had left without finishing the job, meant either he didn't remember his confession of the night before, or he didn't have time to waste.

But he'd be back, for if Thomas could recall the conversation, surely Bernard could as well.

And men willing to destroy one of the noblest groups to have ever existed, merely for personal gain, were men that wouldn't hesitate to kill a friend to preserve the secrets of their crimes.

"Drawer."

Thomas stared at his father. "What, Papa?"

"Drawer."

Thomas rose and rounded his father's desk, pulling open the drawers. He found mostly blank pages, some practice documents, but in the bottom drawer, tucked in the back, he found a carefully wrapped bundle. He removed it and brought it to his father. "Is this it?"

He nodded. "Open."

Thomas opened the bundle and gasped. It was a document with words so shocking, so treasonous, that it must be what Bernard had been talking about. And at the bottom, were the signatures of a dozen men that Thomas was certain were about to die because of it.

His father reached out and pressed a bloody finger against a second page. Thomas quickly read it, tears forming. It was a confession, from his father, to what he had done, and at the bottom were the forged signatures, as proof that he had created the original.

He must have known all along that he was going to die.

He stared at his father. "You knew!"

His father nodded, then reached out, his right hand trembling now. "I'm sorry."

"For what?"

"For leaving you alone."

He shuddered, his eyes closing as one last sigh escaped.

Leaving Thomas alone in a world that preyed on the weak and the innocent.

And those not born privileged enough to live above the law.

Outside Coulommiers, Kingdom of France

Sir Raimond stood at the edge of the clearing, supporting himself with one hand on a tree, as the disturbing scene continued to unfold. A contingent of men was now digging out the mass grave, almost a dozen bodies, and half as many horses, revealed so far. The horses appeared to have been initially wounded by arrows, then put down, some mercy at least shown to the poor creatures.

Who would target horses?

This wasn't a battlefield where desperation might reign. This was the Kingdom of France, a relatively peaceful place where one could usually travel without risk of attack.

And certainly where a delegation of Templar Knights with their sergeants and squires, could travel without fear.

"Notice anything?" he asked of his clerk, standing nearby, his head shaking since they arrived.

"What?"

"The arrows. These were expertly loosed. No brigands did this. Whoever it was, was experienced."

As the dig progressed, they continued to find no evidence of who these men were. He didn't recognize any of them, though he knew who the men in the delegation were supposed to be, and he had never met any of them before. None of them had. There were no surcoats, no crests, no rings or adornments that might suggest who they were.

And the lack of such, suggested they could indeed

be Templars.

But the proof, at least to him, was the fact that every single purse found, contained no more than four *deniers*. And no knight that hadn't taken a vow of poverty, would carry so little on their person.

Nobody buried here wore fancy clothing, or fine leather boots. None showed any evidence of the wealth usually associated with a knight not of the warrior monk orders.

This was the delegation.

He was sure of it.

The number of knights matched what he was expecting, the location was near the route they should have taken, and from what he could tell, they had been killed near the time he would have expected them to arrive.

This was them.

He made the sign of the cross, then turned to his clerk. "Send word that we have found the missing delegation."

The young man bowed, then departed to have messengers dispatched. Raimond returned his attention to his fallen brothers, his chest aching with the senseless loss, wondering why anyone would do such a thing.

It must have been a significant force.

The wounds revealed so far suggested archers and foot soldiers, as well as, most likely, men on horseback. To overwhelm experienced Templar soldiers so completely, would suggest some sort of coordinated surprise attack, an ambush. With the deliberate targeting of the horses, whoever did this obviously wanted to eliminate the ability of their victims to flee the attack.

They wanted them forced to fight in place, on their feet.

Not necessarily a wise move, considering how formidable a Templar Knight could be.

Though if faced with overwhelming odds, there might have been no choice but to surrender.

And the moment they lowered their arms, their fate had been sealed.

And again, he had to ask why.

It must have something to do with this document the men disguised...

He paused, staring at the bodies, his jaw slowly dropping.

Men disguised as Templars had been committing murders.

And these poor souls were missing their surcoats.

Now we know where they got their disguises.

He sighed. He refused to believe these men were killed for their surcoats. These men were missing anything that could link them to the Order, those items either repurposed by those who had attacked them, or buried elsewhere—he had already ordered a search. No documents had been found on them, and they surely would have had many, as they would be carrying letters from the Holy Land for the Pope and the King.

They were killed either for something they carried, or something the attackers thought they carried.

Or to cover something up.

He pursed his lips as he stared at the bodies now lined up neatly side-by-side. Could a document have been in their possession that these men wanted, not because it would incriminate the Templars, but because it would incriminate themselves?

He shook his head in frustration. There was no way to know. These men were dead, unable to answer his questions, and the sole witness was a young boy, whose recollection couldn't be entirely relied upon.

They had to capture those responsible. Only they knew the motive for this horrendous crime.

He just prayed Marcus and his men were successful.

The horses, stripped of anything useful by his men, were set alight, and he backed off, having no desire for his nostrils to be filled with such an unpleasant notion. As he walked away, he did take comfort in one thing.

Those committing the murders were *not* Templars.

Thank God for that.

De Charney Residence
Villeneuve-le-Comte, Kingdom of France

"Are you Sir Everard de Charney?"

The man before Sir Bernard bowed slightly. "I am. And you are?"

"Sir Bernard de Claret." Bernard plunged his dagger into the man's stomach then thrust upward, executing the man in the fashion so successful earlier this morning with Thomas' father. He twisted the blade then pulled it out before stepping back. Everard dropped to a knee, reaching for his own dagger before giving up, his hands instead clasping at his bleeding stomach.

"Why?"

"You are a traitor to the King. Didn't you know?" Bernard produced the document, reading out the text concocted just the night before. "And you signed it!" Bernard took a knee, tapping the man's signature. "See, right there."

Everard stared at the document, confusion dominating his face before he fell to his side, gasping out his final words. "I signed no such document."

Bernard rose as the man's last breath left his body, then leaned over and cleaned his dagger on the man's sleeve.

This does seem to get easier the more you do it.

As he left the home of the last man on his unit's planned route of execution, he felt more satisfied with himself as a man, than he ever had. It was only now that he realized he wasn't a coward compared to the

139

others, he was merely less experienced. He had killed two men now, his face so close he could feel their gasped breath as his blade burrowed into their stomachs, and now, with two kills to his credit, he was a man, a man to be feared, and more importantly, a man to be respected.

He was no longer the nervous, unconfident pathetic excuse of a knight in title only. He *was* a knight, ready to face anyone who would dare challenge him.

Including that disrespectful cretin Valentin, should it be necessary.

He mounted his horse and departed, a shout from inside adding an urgency to his egress, as a servant discovered the body of their master. He noticed some blood on his glove and wiped it on the surcoat, the stain matching the bright red cross emblazoned on the stark white material.

Another murder, committed yet again by a Templar, with witnesses to confirm the deceit.

And with his job done, he headed toward where his unit should be if they had stuck to the plan, now with the excuse of taking care of business, and on his return, eliminating the final name on their list, and in so doing, discovering the very document they had been seeking the entire time.

Proof of the traitorous plans of the Knights Templar, and their supporters within the realm.

Durant Residence
Paris, Kingdom of France

Thomas Durant wasn't certain how long he had sat on the floor, staring at the still form of his dead father, but it was long enough that the sun was now high in the sky, and the bustle on the street in front of their home and business was in full swing.

He let go of his father's cold, stiff hand, then rose, wiping the tears from his face. He stared down at himself, covered in blood, and wasn't sure what to do.

You have to tell someone.

That much was obvious. His father hadn't just died, he had been murdered. And he knew by whom. Yet what could be done? Nobody would believe that nobility had murdered his father. Why would a knight, with royal blood, even visit such a lowly home?

Surely there were witnesses, though. Someone had tended to Bernard's horse for the night, and returned with it the next morning. Surely that person would confirm he had been here.

But a few coins discreetly delivered could change any story in this wretched place.

Nobody would believe him.

He stared at the document his father had prepared for Bernard, and the confession. This was for *him*. This was in case something went wrong. His father wouldn't have written this for himself, he wrote it for a son he knew would be in trouble. Bernard would be coming for him, and nobody would believe him.

But with this forgery, and the confession, someone

just might.

Those named in the document.

They would know they never signed the forgery, and it would be in their best interest to get to the bottom of what was going on. He stared at the names, none of them familiar. He had no way of finding any of them.

And didn't Bernard say they were killing them?

The night was foggy, though he was certain something had been said about these names. But that wasn't of importance. What was, was who they were. And if this document was meant to take down the Templars, then these signatures must belong to Templar Knights.

A sense of relief slowly swept through him as he realized whom he might trust.

And he prayed he was right. For if he weren't, he had nowhere to hide, and Bernard would surely do unto him, as he had done unto his father.

Outside Saint-Augustin, Kingdom of France

Sir Valentin led his men from the town, the third name on their list now eliminated, and for a third time, no incriminating document found. When he had interrogated his prisoner a week ago, he had been assured a second document existed, though it had taken a sustained beating for that admission to be made.

Could he have lied?

It was possible. Perhaps the man had told him what he wanted to hear. He frowned, a rage building within. This entire exercise might prove fruitless should it be based upon a lie, and his assurances to the King of the document's existence could prove not only an embarrassment, but disastrous to his station.

He could lose his post, his family's name could be tarnished, and he could be remembered as the one who brought down his own house through his own arrogance and overconfidence.

For he shared his king's desire to rid the realm of these Templars who wielded far too much power. They were the bank. They were the money. And they were above the law. Their vast holdings in gold, jewels, debt, and property, made them immensely powerful. Kings and nobles borrowed from them, and hefty fees were charged, depending upon the perceived risk.

And backed by the Pope, men like him couldn't touch them.

Another thorn in the side of France.

Why should any of His Highness' subjects be allowed to pledge their loyalty to the Papacy, and not their lawful King? It was intolerable.

So thought the King, and he as well.

Which was why when he found out about the meeting with the delegation from the Holy Land, he had intercepted one of the attendees, and beat him until he had what he wanted.

And a grateful King had given him his blessing.

"Find us this document, and we will forever be in your debt."

To be in a king's debt could mean great things for him and his family. Perhaps marriage into the royal family, perhaps invitation into the court itself.

Great things.

Life changing things.

But so far, no document had been found, and they were quickly running out of people to interrogate.

"Is that Sir Bernard?"

Valentin rose in his saddle and spotted a grinning Bernard standing among the men, men who seemed unusually pleased to see the bumbling fool.

Valentin charged into the crowd, parting it with his horse, then jumped down, his finger jabbing the air between him and the deserter. "Where have you been? You leave here without informing me of where you are going? And you dare return? Tell me now why I shouldn't have you executed for desertion?"

Bernard smiled, holding up a piece of paper. "I have it."

"You have what?"

"What we've been looking for."

Valentin paused, his rage temporarily put on hold as he stared at the paper in Bernard's hand. "Explain."

"I had a family matter to attend to, of a personal nature. I conducted my business yesterday, and on my way back, I decided to deal with Sir Everard de Charney, the last name on our list, as I was passing nearby. I interrogated him, and he produced this document." He handed it to Valentin. "Exactly what we've been looking for, wouldn't you say?"

Valentin quickly read the document, his heart hammering with excitement as he realized the idiot was right. This *was* what they had been looking for. In fact, it was more than they could have hoped for. It was *exactly* what they were looking for. It laid out the Templars' opposition to the King, how they and the Papacy would call the King's loans, and refuse to issue any more credit until additional collateral could be obtained. And without the funds, the King would be forced to capitulate to his enemies, enemies a secret treaty had been signed with between the Papacy and its army, the Knights Templar.

With a dozen signatories, matching those on the previous document they had already obtained.

Thus sealing the fate of the Templars.

He stared at Bernard, shaking his head. "I don't know what to say."

Bernard smiled slightly. "You need say nothing, but know this. The next man that disrespects me, will answer to my blade."

Valentin bowed slightly. "You have earned my respect, and I am sure, the thanks of the King."

"Then I suggest we present him with this document at once, and arrest those who would dare challenge our King!"

Valentin smiled, the change in Bernard obvious. What had happened in the past day, he wasn't sure, but whatever had, it was enough to return to them a changed man, a man he might actually respect.

Yet no matter what had happened, or how he might feel about the man, one thing was certain. This document would please the King, allow the destruction of the Templars, and put his liege in debt to him.

Changing his life forever.

He turned to his men, seeking out his scribe. "I want copies of this made immediately. And I want warrants written for every man on this document. No longer shall we work in the shadows. Send teams to the local Bailiff's Delegates to make the arrests and bring them to Montry, including any Templars that may be with them, for they are traitors to the King. Tomorrow we shall present these parasites to the King himself!"

A roar went up from the men, everyone to a man clearly thrilled their mission had been a success, thanks to the fool thrust upon them by the King doing a favor for someone he obviously owed a great debt to.

And after tomorrow, that favor owed would be to him.

"What of those that are already dead? Surely we don't need to issue warrants for them?"

Valentin smiled at his squire. "You're forgetting one thing."

"Sir?"

"We're not supposed to know they're dead!"

Enclos du Temple, Templar Fortress
Paris, Kingdom of France

Thomas stumbled toward the large fortress at the end of the street. It was an imposing structure, a sign of wealth, power, and stature, the red and white flags fluttering in the stiff breeze identifying who merited such things.

Templars.

This was their European headquarters, and the only place he could be certain to find someone he could trust with the knowledge he alone possessed.

And the murderer, Bernard.

As his memory of the night before continued to return, he couldn't believe this so-called friend had the gall to promise to take care of him should something happen to his father. Had he planned on murdering him last night, or was it decided after the false promise was made?

To think he had been in a good mood this morning, entertaining nothing but kind thoughts about his boyhood friend, when all the while his father bled to death on the floor of their humble shop. He had seen Bernard ride away. If he had been home only a short while earlier, he might have saved his father, yet instead, he had taken his time returning after the cancellation of his work.

Because he was in a good mood. He now had a lifeline should things go terribly wrong.

He had Bernard.

Had.

Thomas had never been a vengeful man. He hadn't experienced enough in life to really feel the urge. He had lost his mother to poor health, not murder. He had always had little, so knew no better, and there was nothing to be envious of in his neighborhood— everyone was destitute.

He hated the gangs that controlled too much, and did feel some resentment when a member of the aristocracy passed through for some reason, though none had ever treated him with disrespect—they simply ignored him as one would an insect.

Nothing had truly enraged him in his life.

Until today.

Today, as the moments since his father's death grew, he became determined to seek justice for his murder. And he knew he was probably incapable of delivering it. Justice was out of the question. Nothing would ever happen to a nobleman for killing a peasant. He would merely claim he was attacked, and that would be the end of it.

No one would doubt the word of a nobleman.

Which was why he needed the help of the men inside this fortress he now stood in front of.

For it was in their interest to help, for their very futures might rely upon it.

He patted the pouch carrying the two documents, then approached one of the guards standing at the gates.

"State your business."

Thomas shuddered at the firmness and confidence of the imposing man's voice. "Umm, I have a document that must be seen by someone in charge."

"What is the nature of this document?"

148

"I-I can show you it, if you want."

The guard nodded, and Thomas produced the forgery. The man's eyes shot wide. "Come with me."

Thomas scrambled to keep up, the man marching through the courtyard toward a large building, with a sense of urgency that with each step gave him more hope. If whomever he was being taken to felt as much urgency, his quest for justice, for vengeance, might just be quenched.

They entered the building and the guard held out a finger, pointing at the floor. "Wait here."

Thomas stopped as the guard showed the forgery to another man, whose eyebrows rose as he read it. He dismissed the guard then beckoned Thomas to follow him, no words exchanged. They went deeper into the bowels of the building, eventually arriving at a set of double doors. Three quick raps and they were inside, the document presented to an elderly man sitting behind a simple desk, his gray beard neatly trimmed, his clothes simple but clean, his Templar tunic a crisp white and unmarred by battle. He read the document, his surprise evident, though less pronounced than the previous two men. He dismissed Thomas' escort, who closed the doors behind him.

"Have a seat."

Thomas took the proffered chair, noticing for the first time that his hands were trembling as he clutched his pouch close to his chest.

"I am Sir Matthew Norris, commander of this facility, and Templar Master for France. And you are?"

"T-Thomas Durant."

"And how did you come to possess this document?"

"My-my father made it."

The man's eyes narrowed. "Made it? Explain."

Thomas stared at the floor, then out the window, as he tried to find the words to explain his father was a criminal, without disrespecting the now dead man.

"Well, boy, out with it!"

Thomas flinched. "Umm, he's a forger, sir."

An audible sigh escaped his interrogator. "So this is a forgery?"

"Yes."

A sign of the cross was made, likely a thanks to God, Sir Matthew obviously having thought it might be genuine. "And what is the purpose of this? Are you here to blackmail us into giving you money in exchange for not releasing it?"

A pit formed in Thomas' stomach and his jaw dropped. "Oh, no! Nothing like that!"

"Then you better explain."

"Perhaps this will help." Thomas produced the confession, handing it to Matthew, who quickly scanned it, his eyes widening.

"Sir Bernard de Claret commissioned this?"

"Yes."

"I've never heard of him, but I've heard of the family, of course. Well connected. So according to this, Sir Bernard had your father create this document, forging the signatures on the bottom from another document that Sir Bernard had in his possession."

"Yes."

"And why isn't your father here to attest to this?"

"Because he's dead, sir. Murdered this very morning by Sir Bernard."

The man frowned, his voice becoming more gentle. "I'm truly sorry for your loss. He shall be in my prayers tonight." He sighed. "What else can you tell me?"

"We made rather merry last night, sir, and Bernard told me that he was doing this to earn his own way, to respect, I guess, instead of relying on his family name. Apparently, he was teased a lot, and disrespected by the others in the King's Personal Guard."

"So destroying the Templars is his solution? Unbelievable."

"Yes, sir, but I think there's more to it than that."

Matthew leaned forward in his chair. "Explain."

"Well, from what I can recall—and forgive me, it is a little fuzzy as I had much to drink—I don't think this was all his idea."

"What do you mean?"

"Well, I think the forgery was his idea, but all he was doing was creating a false copy of a document they were already looking for. My understanding is they are interrogating those men listed, trying to find a document such as this, and executing them when they don't."

Matthew exhaled loudly, leaning back. He tapped the forgery. "Do you recognize any of these names?"

Thomas shook his head. "No."

"Well I do. In fact, I recognize them all. And two on this list are dead already. We received word yesterday of Guy Fabron's murder, along with his wife, and this morning of Sir Gilbert de St. Leger's murder in his chambers. This would seem to lend credence to your story."

"What will you do?"

Matthew raised his voice, shouting for someone, a young man rushing in moments later. He handed him the forgery. "Record these names, then send messengers to them all. Tell them to seek shelter immediately, as their lives may be in danger. Further instructions will follow."

"Yes, sir." The young man quickly wrote down the names then departed.

"Is there anything else you can do? Can you go to the King and explain everything? Have Bernard arrested?"

The Templar grunted. "Son, I don't think you understand what is going on here."

Thomas stared at him, the old man apparently correct.

"Son, Sir Bernard created a forgery of a document he was looking for—the King's Personal Guard, were looking for. The King's Personal Guard do nothing unless ordered to by the King himself."

"So…" Thomas' stomach flipped and his eyes shot wide. "You mean the King ordered them to find this document?"

"Exactly."

"Then what-what are you going to do?"

Matthew sighed. "I'm not sure yet, but if I can't figure out something soon, it may be too late, and none of us may survive the week."

"Surely he couldn't do anything to you! You're the Knights Templar!"

"Son, he's the King, and the King can do pretty much anything he wants as long as he has the tacit support of his court. And a document such as this"— he jabbed a finger at the forgery—"would be enough to secure it."

"But why would he do such a thing? Why would the King want to destroy the Templars?"

"Do you have any idea what we do here?"

Thomas glanced around, then shrugged. "I-I really don't know. I'm sorry. I always thought you defended the Holy Land."

"Yes, but we also control a massive amount of wealth, and lend that money to people, including people like your king."

Thomas' jaw dropped. "The King owes you money?"

"A nearly unfathomable amount. And should he eliminate us...?"

Thomas' jaw dropped. "He won't have to repay what he owes!"

"Exactly."

Thomas shook his head slowly. "Then there's no hope. He'll never listen to anything we say, because there's too much at stake."

"I fear you may be right, my young friend." Matthew rose and Thomas quickly followed. "I suggest you return home and tend to your father. Then I suggest you go somewhere Sir Bernard is unaware of, for I fear he will return to eliminate the last witness to his crime."

Thomas shuddered. "I have nowhere to go. And I will have no man drive me from my home."

Matthew rounded the desk and placed a hand on Thomas' shoulder. "You're a brave lad. I'm sure your father must have been very proud of you." He led him to the door. "If you insist on staying, then leave your address with my clerk, as I may need to call upon you.

May the good Lord protect you."
"And you, sir. All of you."

De Saint-Michel Residence
Mauperthuis, Kingdom of France

Sir Marcus sat in the hall of Sir Olivier de Saint-Michel's home, an impressive affair for the country, this apparently a summer refuge when the nobleman wanted to escape the bustle of Paris. They had arrived last night, and had stood vigil since, awaiting the arrival of those determined to make this Olivier's final resting place.

"You say the delegation from the Holy Land is missing."

Marcus nodded, scratching a well-behaved Tanya behind the ears, the dog proving a good companion. "Sir Raimond said they were overdue. Assuming that hasn't changed, then they must be at least three days late now."

Olivier shook his head. "Impossible. I traveled with them, and they spent the night here just three days ago. They were only half a day's ride from meeting with Sir Raimond."

Marcus frowned. "Then something must have happened to them."

"I can't see anything that could have delayed them from where we parted. Not this long."

Simon grunted. "Unless they were intercepted by a messenger, and changed their plans."

Marcus nodded. "Yes, that is possible. But to not then send a messenger to inform Sir Raimond?" He shook his head. "I can't believe that."

"You're probably right."

Marcus winked at his sergeant. "I'm always right."

Simon gave him a look. "Where's the humility now?"

Olivier laughed. "I envy you, Sir Marcus. The respect and camaraderie you share with your men is something to behold, something I think all men should aspire to, though I fear far too many fail at. I know when the King requires me to raise an army, I try to treat my men with respect, but our stations are so different, and I am taking them from their homes and duties, that I know, despite the façade, that they tolerate me more than anything else."

Marcus wasn't certain what to say to that without confirming what the man was saying. "Things are different in the Order. I have no wealth or power for my men to be jealous or envious of, and beyond a title, I have little more than those who would serve under me. In fact, my sergeant and squires may possess more worldly goods than I, as their vows are far less restrictive than mine." He grinned at Simon and the others. "I should be envious of them, should the good Lord not tell me different."

His squire, David, perched near the window as a lookout, inhaled quickly.

"What is it?"

"Riders. Four of them, coming down the path."

"This could be it." Marcus rose and straightened his armor. "Are they wearing our markings?"

David shook his head. "No. It looks like the King's Personal Guard."

Marcus exchanged a puzzled glance with Simon, then turned to Olivier. "Do you have business with the King that might bring these men?"

Olivier shook his head. "None that would require his guard. Messengers, of course, arrive all the time, but never the guard, and never four."

Tanya growled, and Marcus signaled for her to stay, then strode toward the door. "Then let us see what their business is."

David opened the door and Marcus stepped through, followed by Simon then Olivier. The four riders came to a halt just short of the welcoming party, two of them dismounting.

Marcus stepped forward. "What is your business here?"

The man apparently in charge produced a document. "By order of His Majesty the King, I have a warrant for the arrest of Sir Olivier de Saint-Michel, as well as any and all Templars with him."

Marcus' eyebrows rose slightly at the last part, motioning for Simon and his squires to hold their ground, all three bristling with the implications. "And what are the charges?"

"Treason against the King."

Olivier gasped. "Nonsense! I am loyal to the King. He knows that."

A second document was produced and held out. "This is proof of your crime. A copy of what was discovered."

Marcus took the document and read it, his chest tightening and his stomach quickly becoming unsettled. It was definitely a treasonous affair if this declaration were true. He showed it to Olivier, who quickly scanned it.

"I've never seen this before in my life."

"Is that not your name on the bottom?"

"Yes, my name, but not my signature."

"This is but a copy. The original is in safekeeping, and possesses the signatures of those involved in this conspiracy to overthrow the King. You will all come with us."

Marcus ignored him, instead turning to Olivier. "You've never seen this before?"

"Never! I swear!"

Marcus quickly scanned the names at the bottom of the document. They matched exactly those on the genuine document he had already seen summarizing the meeting. "These are the same men who signed the agreed upon summary of your meeting last week, agreed?"

Olivier nodded. "Yes. I did sign *that* document."

"And nothing of this nature was discussed there?"

"Of course not! That would be treasonous! We merely brought the delegation up to date on what had happened since they left the Holy Land, so they would be prepared for their meeting with the King and his representatives. Nothing calling for his overthrow was discussed. Nothing of the sort!"

Marcus turned back to the knights facing them. "I would suggest that this is a forgery, and your charges unfounded, especially considering somebody has been murdering the men named on this list."

The man shifted from one foot to the other, glancing away for a second. "I would know nothing of that. I have my orders, and I intend to fulfill them."

"Under whose command do you serve?"

"That is not your concern. I serve the King. You *will* come with us. Now."

Marcus shook his head. "This man is under *my*

protection. Since someone has been killing the men on this list, I cannot take the risk that you aren't those responsible. Tell us where to bring him, and you have my word as a Templar Knight, that he shall be delivered."

"That is unacceptable. You and your men will surrender your arms, or face the consequences."

Marcus smiled. "It wouldn't end well for you, I assure you."

The man stepped back and drew his sword, his companions doing the same. Marcus remained still, holding out a hand slightly to his left, steadying his men. "Are you sure you want to do this? I went to confession this morning, and my conscience is clear, my soul prepared for death. Are yours?"

"Will you surrender?"

"No."

"Then die!"

The man charged forward and an arrow pierced his chest as Jeremy's aim was quick and true. Marcus drew his sword, pushing Olivier back toward the door as he parried a blow from the second dismounted man. Simon thrust his sword through the gasping commander, removing him from the threat list as Tanya barked in the background, the closed door preventing her from getting in the way.

Another arrow was loosed, one of the soldiers on horseback crying out as he grabbed for his shoulder. Marcus stepped past the body of the commander and thrust his blade toward his prey, catching him on the side and deflecting off the chainmail. The man swung for a counterattack and Marcus pulled back, angling his sword to block the blow, the two blades sparking as they slid against each other. He snapped a kick at the man's groin, his boot catching his opponent's nether region, enough to have him double over momentarily. Marcus kneed him in the face, breaking his nose, blood spurting as he fell onto his back.

Marcus stepped over him, pointing at the now prone man, Simon finishing him off as Marcus rushed the two men still on horseback. He reached up for the wounded man and hauled him off his steed as the other turned away, urging his horse toward a hasty retreat. As Marcus dropped his sword and pulled his dagger, Jeremy rushed forward with David, both sending arrows arcing through the air, one hitting with a satisfying thud, the second a moment later, the rider falling backward in his saddle, then onto the gravel path.

And with a final thrust, Marcus buried his dagger to the hilt, the last of the four men sent to meet their maker.

Or His fallen angel.

Marcus stood, surveying the scene, the four men sent to arrest them dead, there no mercy on the battlefields of the Holy Land, and no quarter shown here today.

It was unfortunate.

A distinctive sound he had heard too many times on the battlefield had him spinning and shielding Olivier. "Take cover!"

Jeremy cried out as the impact of the arrow was heard. Marcus looked to see his squire grabbing at his shoulder, the cloth torn, a bloody gash visible, the arrow responsible lying on the ground behind him.

A horse whinnied, and they all turned to see a lone

rider racing away, a fifth man they hadn't known was there.

"Should I pursue?" asked Simon, already reaching for one of the horses.

"No, he has too much of a lead, and we don't know what awaits us out there. He could have friends, and then we'll lose you to an ambush."

"Then what should we do? We can't stay here. They'll claim we murdered four of the King's Guard."

"Didn't we?" asked David as he tended to Jeremy's wound. "I mean, we *did* just kill four of the guard, issuing a lawful warrant."

Marcus nodded. "Indeed we did." He stepped over the body of the leader, retrieving the warrant and the copy of what Olivier insisted was a forgery. He quickly read the warrant, then turned to Jeremy. "How is he?"

"He'll live. Nothing serious, but he should take it easy until it heals."

Jeremy grunted. "Nonsense. It just grazed me. Nothing like what happened to you, sir."

Marcus rotated his left shoulder, the pain now making itself evident, the brief battle unfortunately aggravating what he had almost forgotten about. "This is true, but I am an exceptional warrior."

"Handsome too," added Simon.

"Indeed. To compare yourself to me, is, well, a ridiculous notion."

"I don't know what I was thinking," grimaced Jeremy. "May I get on my knees and kiss your royal ass, or is someone already in line?"

Marcus roared with laughter. "He'll be all right. But I want you to return to the farm."

Jeremy struggled to his feet, despite the

protestations of David. "No, sir, I'll be fine."

Marcus waved his hand, cutting off the debate. "No. If we run into more trouble, you could get yourself killed. Besides, if they are arresting Templars, I'm concerned about the farm and the children. They may seek us out there, and I'd like someone to be there to protect them. Can I count on you to do that?"

Jeremy's chest swelled and his shoulders squared. "Yes, sir. It would be an honor to protect your family."

"Good, then it is settled. David, prepare his horse after you've bandaged him up."

"Yes, sir."

Marcus turned to Olivier. "And you, sir. Is there some place you can go until we get to the bottom of this?"

"Yes. I'll head north to my cousin's. They'll be able to protect me there, and receive news of any goings on at the court." He extended a hand, and Marcus took it. "Thank you, sir, thank you all for saving my life. I am in your debt."

Marcus bowed slightly. "No debt is ever owed for a Templar doing his duty. Now I suggest you hurry."

"Of course, of course." Olivier opened the door, and a frantically barking Tanya erupted from inside, nearly bowling the man over. She quickly circled the bodies, seeking more to battle, then rushed to Marcus' side, jumping up with excited energy. He laughed, patting her as he tried to calm her down.

"It's all right, girl, it's all over. I know you wanted to help us, but you could have been hurt." He dropped to a knee and delivered some well-received scratches, then turned to Jeremy. "I want you to take her with you. She'll serve as good protection for you on your journey alone, and then for the children once you reach the farm."

Jeremy nodded, then winced when David tied off the bandage. "Yes, sir. I think that's a good idea."

Marcus stood, Simon joining him, having finished searching the bodies and horses. "Anything?"

Simon shook his head. "Nothing of interest."

"No Templar surcoats?"

Simon grunted. "No. Which means whoever has been impersonating us is still out there."

"Yes, and now there is a witness out there who saw this skirmish, where four Templars apparently murdered four of the King's Guard trying to do their duty."

Simon sighed. "I think we're in it deep now, sir."

"Indeed. I think it's time we sought counsel."

"But who could be more wise than you?"

Marcus chuckled. "None, I am sure, though I was thinking Sir Raimond might be able to provide some sage advice."

Archambault held up a finger, halting the latest interruption as he battled a pounding headache. The past days had been as hectic as any he could recall since agreeing to be the Bailiff's Delegate for the village, and he was now regretting the choice, the small stipend hardly worth the constant barrage of questions from concerned citizens.

Though he didn't blame his neighbors. They were scared, and concerned. A husband and wife were dead, murdered in their very home, possibly by Templars.

And if one couldn't trust Templars, then whom could one trust?

He had checked on young Pierre this morning on his way in, and was pleased to see he was in good spirits. If Sir Marcus hadn't agreed to take him in, he feared things would be much worse for the boy. The two young orphaned children were making things much easier on the lad, and the beautiful Mistress Isabelle was doing a smashing job in taking care of them.

It's too bad Sir Marcus is a Templar. They would make a good match.

He feared Marcus was taking on more than he fathomed when he had decided to remain here and raise his late sister's children, and word had arrived only moments ago from Paris that there were no living relations for Pierre to be sent to stay with.

He was alone in this cruel world.

Perhaps Sir Marcus will take him in as well.

He sighed, the idea ridiculous, though he feared it was the only hope the little boy had for a happy future.

He finally opened his eyes and looked up at the new arrival, nearly soiling himself. Four of the King's Personal Guard stood in his tiny office, a large crowd already gathered outside to see what was afoot. He rose, his entire body trembling. "Gentlemen, what can I do for you?"

"We have an arrest warrant for Mr. Guy Fabron. Where can I find him?"

Archambault's jaw dropped, his eyes widening. "Surely you jest, good sir! Why would anyone want to arrest Mr. Fabron? He's an auditor, here on behalf of His Majesty!"

"He is a traitor to the King, as are his accomplices. I have orders to arrest him at once, and any Templars that may be with him."

"Templars! Why Templars?"

"They are traitors. Evidence has been found that shows they and others, including Mr. Fabron, have been conspiring to overthrow the King. Now, I will ask you one last time, where can we find Mr. Fabron?"

Archambault stared, not sure of what to do, still attempting to process everything that had just been said. Mr. Fabron a traitor? Templars trying to overthrow the King? It was all too fantastic, yet these four men looked like they considered the charges serious, and appeared to have no patience.

And one didn't risk the ire of the King's Personal Guard.

"He-he's dead."

The man stared at him. "Excuse me?"

"He's dead. Along with his wife. They were both murdered."

"By whom?"

"Possibly Templars, or men disguised as Templars."

The man exchanged glances with the others, a slight smirk revealed on one's face. "I would suggest the former. He was most likely murdered by Templars to cover up their own treachery."

"Unbelievable!" hissed Archambault. "We, umm, have Templars in town. They just arrived this week."

The man's eyes narrowed. "What is their business here?"

"The knight, Sir Marcus de Rancourt, was from the area originally. His sister recently died, leaving her two children orphaned. He returned with three others, and has decided to remain and raise the children."

"Where can I find these men?"

Archambault shook his head. "I don't know. They left yesterday to try and find out who murdered Mr. Fabron."

The man grunted. "Probably fleeing the scene of the crime. I will require proof of Mr. Fabron's death, then we will be on our way."

"Yes, sir."

Archambault led them outside where the bits and pieces of the overheard conversation were already being repeated and distorted, but he would deal with that later. He quickly led them to where the two bodies had been cleaned and sewn up in canvas in preparation for their return to Paris later today. He pointed at Mr. Fabron. "Did you want it opened?"

The man shook his head. "No, I wouldn't recognize him regardless. Do you swear this is the body of Mr. Fabron?"

"I do."

A paper was presented. "Then sign here."

He signed the paper, and the men left, leaving him to deal with what was quickly turning into an outraged mob. He walked into the midst of them, holding his hands up in a failing effort to calm them. "People, please, listen to me, and I will explain what has just happened."

"I'll tell you what happened. Those Templars murdered a government official, and now Hell's fury will come down upon us!"

Archambault's chest tightened as those surrounding roared in agreement. "Now, now, please, calm down. That is *not* what is happening here. The men who just left had a warrant for the arrest of Mr. Fabron, not the Templars."

"That's not true!" shouted someone in the back. "I heard him say that he was here to arrest any Templars that might be with Mr. Fabron. If they're so innocent, then why would they be arresting Templars?"

"And I heard him say that Templars were plotting to overthrow the King!"

It was clear that there was nothing he could say to calm these people. They were quoting things he couldn't deny. The man *had* said Mr. Fabron was conspiring with Templars to overthrow the King, and it was well known among his fellow citizens, that young Pierre had seen Templars commit the dastardly deed.

He couldn't deny any of it.

"We need to remain calm, and let justice prevail!" he finally said, shouting overtop the others. "Mr. Fabron is dead, and his body will be gone before nightfall. If what has been said is true about the Templars, then let Paris deal with it. They will arrest them, and justice will be delivered. And should they not, then we will know that this has all been a horrible misunderstanding, and everyone will move on with their lives. But for now, it is essential we not give in to irrational fear. None of us has done anything wrong, therefore none of us has anything to worry about. Let Paris figure this out, and continue on with our day."

"I, for one, will never trust Paris to have our best interests at heart!" shouted someone. "And should they find the Templars guilty, could the King not take his wrath out on us for giving safe harbor to four of these traitors?"

"That's right! This new knight isn't one of us. His men aren't even from around here. Why should we put our lives at risk for outsiders? I say we get rid of them now, so that when the King's men return, they will see we are loyal to His Majesty, and show no quarter to those who would betray him!"

A roar of approval erupted from the crowd, and Archambault knew all was lost.

"Burn the farm!" was shouted by someone, the chant taken up by the crowd as they turned, abandoning Archambault, instead heading for the family farm outside of the village, where three young children and their caregiver lived, defenseless.

And he knew, if he tried to stop them, he too might feel their wrath.

Instead, he returned to his small office and closed

the door, saying a silent prayer for the little ones, and the fetching young lady he had hoped might make a good wife to Sir Marcus, a knight whom until now, he had the utmost respect for.

Yet with what he had heard earlier, he now had doubts about his motives.

Was he here for his sister and her children?

Was he even the brother of Nicoline?

His jaw dropped at the thought. They had no proof beyond the letter. Could he have intercepted it and taken on Sir Marcus' identity? Could he have been sent to murder Mr. Fabron?

He sighed, closing his eyes and gripping his pounding skull.

Please, Lord, let this all be the horrible imaginings of a troubled soul.

But he feared the truth lay somewhere between his musings, and the charges levied earlier.

Though regardless of the truth, there was one thing about to happen that shouldn't, and that he could do nothing about.

Four innocent souls were about to have their lives torn apart at a minimum, and forfeited, at worst.

Templar Commandry
Coulommiers, Kingdom of France

"A messenger arrived less than an hour ago from the headquarters in Paris. The news is disturbing and difficult to believe, but would seem to be borne out by what you have just told me."

Sir Marcus sat across from Sir Raimond, Simon beside him, David attending the horses. They had ridden hard to get here, and he had to admit, he was tired, months of little training or action leaving him less of a man, less of a knight.

It disturbed him.

Am I to become soft in this new life I've chosen?

The answer seemed rather obvious, though farming was not an easy life. But neither was that of a warrior monk. Constant training, constant prayer, with little reward beyond the love of one's brothers and one's Lord Jesus Christ. It had always been enough, and he prayed that life on the farm, with the children, would be as well.

Though now he feared if that would even be an option left open to him after today's events.

"What did this messenger have to say?"

Raimond tapped the copy of the document proving the Templars' treasonous wishes. "This is a fake."

Marcus' eyebrows rose slightly. "Obviously, but what proof did this messenger provide?"

"The forger is dead, murdered by the man who

commissioned the document. His son survived, and brought a copy of the forgery, along with a confession from the forger, to our headquarters in Paris."

Marcus glanced at Simon. "He must have known he was going to die. Did this boy say who had his father create the document?"

"He did indeed. Sir Bernard de Claret."

"Never heard of him. Is he important?"

Raimond grunted. "Only through his family name. Word is that he is considered a bit of a joke in official circles. Not very well respected, merely tolerated because of the family's status."

Marcus sighed. "It would appear that someone has decided they want to prove their worth to those who would mock him."

Simon shifted in his seat. "And our Order is to pay the price."

Marcus agreed. "He must be stopped."

Raimond nodded. "Obviously, but how? There's something else I haven't told you, that I have to assume is connected. We found the missing delegation from the Holy Land this morning. Or rather, I think we did."

Marcus eyed him. "You think? Wouldn't they know who they are?"

Raimond frowned. "We found their bodies. They were found buried with several of their horses outside of town, in a clearing in the forest."

Marcus gasped, making the sign of the cross. "This is unbelievable! But you said you *think* it's them. What do you mean?"

"They were stripped of any markings that might have identified them. Tunics, surcoats. Anything."

171

"Then why do you think it's them?"

"There were three knights plus the proper number accompanying them, and they were found near a route that would have led them here. Judging by the state of their bodies, it would suggest they were ambushed by a substantial force that included archers, a few days ago."

"That would suggest they are indeed the delegation."

"All that would, but I think the most convincing piece of evidence is what they *did* have on their person, rather than what they did not."

"And that was?"

Raimond reached into a drawer and produced half a dozen purses, tossing them on the desk. "None had more than four *deniers* on their person, and we all know who can carry no more than this pittance of an amount."

Marcus sighed, any doubt he might have had, wiped away. "Templar Knights sworn to poverty."

Simon growled, shifting again in his seat as if he were struggling to contain himself. "Who would do such a thing?"

Raimond shook his head. "It would appear this Sir Bernard is definitely involved. Who, beyond that, I do not know."

Marcus scratched his chin. "You said they had been stripped of their surcoats and tunics."

"Yes."

"Well, I think we can safely assume that this is where those posing as Templars found their stolen clothes."

"Such disrespect," muttered Simon. "They deserve

to burn in Hell."

Raimond nodded. "God will judge them when given His chance. I feel confident your desire will be fulfilled."

Marcus leaned forward. "So, we know that Sir Bernard had the forgery created. What we don't know is whom he is working for, and whom he is working with. We know at least three men are involved, as we know three were involved in the murder of Mr. Fabron."

"More than that," said Simon. "There is no way three men were able to wipe out our delegation so easily. They must have had a substantial force. Even surprise wouldn't level the odds of three against a dozen."

Marcus nodded. "Agreed. If they had archers, and enough men to overwhelm our delegation, then they must be well funded."

Raimond held up the letter from Paris. "With Sir Bernard involved, we know at least some segment of nobility is involved. We need to find out whom he is working for, or with."

A thought occurred to Marcus, and he leaned forward, grabbing the warrant issued for Sir Olivier de Saint-Michel's arrest. He scanned it and smiled, holding up the warrant for the others to see. "We've had the answer sitting in front of us this entire time."

Raimond stared at him. "Who?"

Marcus pointed at the signature at the bottom of the warrant. "The man who issued the warrant. Sir Valentin de Vaux."

Raimond's eyes bulged. "Do you have any idea whom that is?"

Marcus tensed. "No, but I get the distinct impression that you do."

"He's the head of the King's Personal Guard."

Marcus suppressed the urge to curse. "If that's the case, then there can be only one person behind this."

Simon didn't suppress the urge, though quickly followed it with a sign of the cross. "The King himself."

Raimond's shoulders sank. "What can we possibly do to stop this?"

Marcus rose, the others following. "We must find out where they are taking those they are arresting, for that is where we will find our conspirators."

Simon stared at him. "And then what?"

"We do whatever it takes to make them confess to their crimes."

"What good would that do?"

Marcus lifted the copy of the forgery. "You're forgetting one thing."

Simon threw up his hands. "Obviously, otherwise I'd sound as confident as you now do!"

Marcus smiled, Raimond failing to suppress a snort. "*If* they had intended to create a forgery, then they wouldn't have been looking for the genuine article all this time. They would have just created it, then issued their warrants. But that's not at all what happened."

Raimond's eyes widened. "Someone doesn't know what's going on."

"Exactly!"

Simon stared at them both. "I'm still in the dark. Somebody, please shine a light!"

"Don't you see? Sir Bernard had the forgery created yesterday. The arrest warrants were issued only today. That means that he, either alone or in concert with others, decided a forgery was necessary to achieve their goals, goals issued to them most likely by the King. If we can show that their proof is indeed a forgery, then we can perhaps convince the King that this entire conspiracy is fake, that we are no threat to his rule, and save the Order from arrest and possible dissolution."

"So how do we find out where they are taking the prisoners?" asked Simon.

"A good question, that perhaps you, Sir Raimond, might be able to find out for us."

"How?"

"Send men at once to all of the towns where these arrests are being made. Someone will know where they were taken. At a very minimum, they will have a direction to follow that will eventually lead to the location. Once we have it, we can intervene, and hopefully, with a little luck and the good Lord's graces, we will be able to preserve the Order from this shameful undertaking."

Approaching Crécy-la-Chapelle, Kingdom of France

Jeremy thanked God once again for creating the magnificent creature now carrying him home. He was exhausted, his wound continuing to seep, and he couldn't wait to reach the farm and lie down, hopefully to the sweet ministrations of the lovely Isabelle Leblanc. She was beautiful, of that, there was no doubt, and she was not for him.

Women like that didn't marry squires.

He would soon have his opportunity to be promoted to sergeant, the order not requiring noble blood for that position, though with his decision to remain here with Sir Marcus, those plans were now on hold, perhaps permanently.

Staying here would never have occurred to him a few days ago. Though neither would leaving Marcus' side. He had served the man faithfully for the better part of a decade, and even if offered the rank of sergeant, he doubted he would accept it unless he could remain with Marcus.

But that would be selfish and self-serving, and not in what was the best interests of the Order, and by extension, his Lord. No, if he were to become a sergeant, he would be issued his black surcoat and tunic, with its large red cross, then be reassigned, perhaps to never see his friends again.

For they were friends.

David was as close to a brother a man could have without sharing a mother, and while Simon outranked him, he thought of him as an older brother, to be respected and obeyed, though still a friend. Marcus by rank could not be considered a brother, even an elder brother—to equate himself with a knight was simply too ridiculous to contemplate.

But Marcus always treated him with respect, was always friendly when possible, though expected his best when on the battlefield. Jeremy always made certain he did the best job possible, giving Marcus no reason to be cross with him, as did David, rarely a raised word heard among the four of them.

A father.

That was how Jeremy thought of Marcus. His guardian and his father. The man he would seek advice from if he were uncertain of what to do, and the man he could always count on to be there for him should the need arise.

And like a good son, Jeremy would be there for him in his time of need in this new home.

Home.

It was a funny way of thinking of the farm. In his thoughts, that is what he was calling it, though for him the Holy Land would always be home, despite the recent defeats suffered at the hands of the unholy Muslims. But home, in reality, was wherever his brothers were, wherever his pseudo-family was.

And now, with Marcus remaining here, on the farm, this was to be his home. Perhaps he would be fortunate enough to meet a young peasant woman and settle down, have some children of his own. Or perhaps, in time, he might head out on his own and rejoin the Order, though the chances of that were slim.

The farm seemed peaceful, and though they had

only spent two nights there so far, he could see it becoming comfortable. It was larger than most in the area, Marcus' late brother-in-law nobility, and though not rich, he wasn't impoverished like most. They had a quaint home with multiple rooms and actual glass on the windows, and a separate barn for the animals, unlike many of their neighbors who slept in the same one-room home with theirs.

This wouldn't be an unpleasant experience, especially if barracks were constructed for them to sleep in, separate from the animals. A bed to call his own, a full belly with plenty to drink, and days filled with purpose, were all a man could hope for these days. As a member of the Order, despite his rank, the excesses in life were frowned upon, and rarely partaken in. He had never bedded a woman, had been drunk only a handful of times, and had never owned anything of value.

How could life here be any worse?

He spotted the town, Tanya recognizing it and charging ahead, barking with excitement. He laughed, then winced, reaching for his shoulder and pressing against it, trying to stem the pain.

Marcus had been right. Returning to the farm was the right decision, and he was thankful it had been made. Should his master have needed him in battle, he would have been useless, and might have ended up putting the lives of everyone at risk. He was confident David could take care of them both should the need arise, though if anything happened to them, Jeremy knew he'd forever blame himself for getting injured.

You should have been paying more attention.

He frowned at his second-guessing. Nobody

expected there to be a fifth man hiding in the trees. Even Marcus had considered the battle finished.

Yes, but Marcus reacted first, and shielded the man you were there to protect. You just caught the arrow.

It could have been worse. A sliced open arm from the grazing of an arrow was much better than what Marcus had suffered in their last battle together. He would make a full recovery, where his master might not, though if there were any doubts whether Marcus was still a formidable warrior, they were put to rest only hours ago when he had bested several healthy soldiers.

He spotted the farm ahead, and urged his horse slightly faster, a shot of excitement giving him strength, and the sight of the beautiful Isabelle hanging laundry, a vision that would better any man's day.

Tanya raced ahead, drawing Isabelle's attention first, the three children rushing out of the house with excitement. Isabelle spotted him coming down the path, and instead of a wave, planted her fists firmly on her hips, an expression displayed that would make most men shrivel.

He did.

He dismounted with a wince.

"And why are you alone? Where are the others?"

"Their business isn't finished. I was—"

Isabelle threw her hands up in frustration. "How much longer am I to be expected to watch over these children? I have my own chores to do, you know."

"I'm sure it won't be—"

"And you, why have you returned alone?" Tanya sniffed at Isabelle. "And why in all that is holy would you bring this wretched creature with you!"

"I was wounded in battle…"

Off the horse and on his own two feet for the first time in hours, the world began to spin. He reached out to steady himself, but his horse betrayed him, stepping aside, leaving Jeremy to collapse onto the ground.

Isabelle yelped, apparently noticing his bleeding arm for the first time. "Children, help me get him inside!"

A flurry of little hands were on him, and he tried to help, forcing himself to a knee, then with the help of Isabelle, to his feet. He stumbled inside, his good arm over her shoulders, then sat in a chair, the relief almost overwhelming.

"Jacques, fetch me fresh water. Angeline, fresh cloths. Pierre, stoke the fire."

The three children bolted in different directions to execute their orders, as Isabelle carefully untied the knot holding the bandage in place, then unwrapped the wound. She hissed at the sight. "This is bad."

Jeremy glanced at the wound. "Not too bad. It will need to be cauterized. Have you ever done that before?"

"Of course not! We're civilized here. I suppose you have cauterized hundreds?"

"Not hundreds, but dozens, yes."

She paused, her cheeks flushing. "You've seen battle that many times?"

Jeremy shook his head. "No." She seemed disappointed. "More. I've only *treated* dozens."

Water and cloth arrived, and she wiped around the wound. She drew Jeremy's dagger and handed it to Pierre. "Put the blade in the fire. Be careful." Pierre complied as Angeline stared at the bloody arm.

Isabelle looked at her. "Do you want to watch, so you know what to do in the future should some fool come to your door requiring assistance?"

Angeline nodded, stepping closer, Jeremy impressed the sight of blood didn't frighten the girl.

"First, you must clean the wound so we can see what we're dealing with." She continued, the children all leaning in to see the still oozing cut. Isabelle handed Pierre a cloth. "Wrap this around the handle of the dagger so you don't hurt yourself. See if the blade is red."

He took the cloth and appeared a moment later with a glowing blade.

Jeremy gulped.

He had done this before, too many times before, but never had he experienced it himself. Though judging from the reactions of the men he had treated, what was to come would be horrific. He grabbed one of the cloths then looked at Isabelle. "Do you know what to do?"

"Of course not, we've already covered this."

"I'm sorry, you were doing so well, I just assumed—"

"Everything to this point has been common sense!"

Jeremy chuckled, though it was more the result of nervous tension than anything else. "Just pick an angle that will cover the entire wound if possible, then when the blade is no longer glowing red, press it against the wound and count to two, then remove it. Repeat this until you've sealed the entire wound. Don't do any area more than two counts, or it could become infected. Questions?"

"Will it hurt?"

"Like nothing you've ever experienced. I will probably cry out, I may even pass out. Just do what I told you, and I'll be fine. Understood?"

Isabelle nodded. She held up the dagger, the red glow already faded. "All right, children, step back." They did, and Isabelle positioned the blade parallel to the wound, only an inch away from Jeremy's skin. "Are you ready?"

He shoved the cloth into his mouth and bit down on it. He nodded.

She pressed down on the wound and the pain wasn't as bad as he had expected.

For barely a moment.

He screamed against the cloth, his teeth clamping down on the material as his eyes bulged and his skin hissed. The children retreated, Angeline crying, when he heard "two" then felt immediate relief.

Then he passed out.

It must have only been for a few moments, because he felt Isabelle's hand gently slapping his cheek, her sweet, concerned voice asking if he was all right. Abruptly the world came into focus. The boys were standing nearby, their eyes wide. Angeline was still crying, and Isabelle was standing in front of him, her hand on his cheek.

"Are you all right?"

He nodded, sucking in a few lungsful of air before taking a look at his arm. He smiled. It was cauterized, the bleeding stopped, and it appeared she had executed her duty almost perfectly, the burn not so bad as to expect infection. He grinned at her. "Perfect!

182

I couldn't have done better myself."

She stood, appearing pleased with herself. She jabbed a finger in his face. "Don't you dare make me do that again!" She stepped back and took Angeline in her arms to comfort the poor girl. "You lot will be the death of me. Here I was, just trying to do—"

"What's that?"

Tanya growled at the door, everyone turning toward the open window, the sound of horses and a crowd of people outside, shouting. Jeremy rose, unable to make out what was being yelled, though despite not hearing the words, the tone was clear.

Whoever it was, they were angry.

And there were a lot of them.

He cautiously approached the window and suppressed a gasp, dozens outside, many with pitchforks and torches, several on horseback, their faces red with anger.

And he could hear their words.

"Burn the farm!"

And even more disturbing was the other chant he could now make out clearly.

"Death to the Templars!"

He spun toward Isabelle. "Is there a back door?"

She nodded, the fear she should be feeling, evident on her face. "Yes."

"Take the children, and get out of here. Don't look back, just run!"

She gathered the children, all now trembling with fear, tears streaking their faces, then turned to look at Jeremy. "What about you?"

"I have to stop them."

"But how? You're wounded!"

"Never mind me. It's my duty to protect you and my master's property. Go, now, so I don't have to worry about you!"

Isabelle stared at him for a moment, then pushed the children through the door and out of sight. He was still wearing most of his chainmail, and his skill being with the bow, his arms were normally free of things that could obstruct their full range of motion.

Hence his earlier wound, that would have glanced off the others' armor.

He looked about for his bow and arrows, and suppressed a curse when he realized they were still on his horse. Tanya was barking now, in a frenzy to get outside and see what was the matter. He peered through the window one last time and saw the torches already pressed into service against the barn.

And now several others were heading for the house. He yanked the door open and surged through, rushing toward his horse, thankfully tied up by one of the children. He grabbed his quiver and slung it over his shoulder, then snatched his bow as he scanned the area, his experienced eye assessing the threat.

These were all peasants, probably whipped up into a frenzy by recent events. There were no archers among them, so if he could hold them off, he might yet save the house.

He stepped out from behind the horse, drawing his first arrow and taking aim. Eyes bulged as those approaching noticed him for the first time. He placed an arrow in the chest of the first, then the second, those with him roaring as they charged him. He had been in enough battles to know it was their shouts that were fueling their courage, nothing more, and he loosed two more arrows, thinning their number enough that those that remained finally realized they were too few for mob-courage to sustain them.

They dropped their torches and ran.

Two men on horseback, swords drawn, charged toward him. He drew another arrow and placed one in the shoulder as the other neared. There'd be no time to take him down.

Suddenly Tanya bolted past him and leaped through the air, her jaws clamping down on the man's arm. He cried out in agony as his sword fell and Tanya dragged him from his saddle and onto the ground. Jeremy ignored his pleas for mercy as he rushed forward, placing his final two arrows into those still at the barn, some not having noticed the skirmish at the residence. Those that remained turned, and when they saw more than half a dozen of their own down, and one of their leaders begging for help as Tanya continued to tear at him, they scattered.

Jeremy rushed toward the barn, the screams of the animals inside heartbreaking. He opened the doors and threw them aside, then quickly opened the stalls, smacking the animals on their behinds, urging them through the smoke and flames. Hooves pounded, cows protested, and pigs squealed as chickens squawked, Jeremy pressing all the way to the back to make certain none were left behind. His eyes burned, as did his lungs, and he gasped for breath as the flames surrounded him. He listened for any more panicked creatures, pushing into each of the stalls, making his way forward, when he was finally overwhelmed, collapsing to his knees.

He crawled toward the door, lost in the smoke, only a hint of daylight making it through the thick, black hatred billowing around him, when someone grabbed his arm. They dragged him toward the door, and it was enough for him to continue his fight, clawing at the ground with his free hand, the light getting brighter, as his world continued to fade around him as he gasped, desperate for air.

Finally, he felt the beginning of relief, the light now bright, the heat behind him, the sounds of the roaring flame dying, a coughing fit clearing his lungs of the deadly soot and ash he had been sucking in.

He flipped on his back, staring up at the sky, his chest heaving, when Tanya's snout appeared, sniffing at him, then licking away at his face.

He continued to cough, then rolled over, retching, a black paste spit up onto the ground. He repeated the process for a few moments before he could finally breathe relatively normal again. He pushed to his knees and stared at the inferno in front of him, the barn a total loss, but the animals, strewn about the property, saved by his actions.

He turned to Tanya and gave her a hug, patting her hard on the side, giving thanks to his own savior, the good Lord's payback for his good deed swift and effective.

Templar Commandry
Coulommiers, Kingdom of France

"Do you miss it?"

Sir Raimond nodded slowly at Sir Marcus' question, asked as this man had served for many years in the Holy Land, and had been gone for some time.

A prospect now faced by Marcus and his men.

"I do, and I don't." Raimond smiled. "I know that's hard to explain." He motioned at their surroundings. "Here, I interact every day with our brothers, most passing through, some who work here every day like I. Until these recent events, I never feared for my life, and never walked the streets of my new home with any worry of attack or molestation. But this unease is nothing compared to the constant vigil necessary in the Holy Land, where a crazed Saracen could attack at any moment. Here, life is a dream compared to there, if only in this small way."

"I sense your answer isn't complete."

Raimond smiled. "And you'd be right. While I love the peace and quiet of this good town, and don't miss the random violence of the Holy Land, I do miss the streets. To walk where Jesus walked, to gaze upon the same skies as the Apostles." He trembled as if covered in goosebumps. "It is something I dearly miss."

Marcus nodded, exchanging a glance with Simon, who he knew felt the same way. "I fear this is what I shall miss as well. Serving my Lord in battle was always an honor, though I must admit, with my growing age, it is no longer the thing of joy I once felt

187

in my youth. I will miss my brothers, though with Simon and the others with me, I think I can tolerate that."

Simon grunted. "Thank you. I think."

Raimond chuckled. "You are fortunate there. Your men have shown tremendous loyalty in deciding to remain with you. This, I think, will ease the transition. When I came here, I knew no one. I relied on the brotherhood of the Order to comfort me to some extent, but mostly on my faith. Both helped me transition to this new life, and though I miss the Holy Land, I now consider this my home. It is a good life, and while it breaks my heart to say it, I think our days in the Holy Land are numbered."

Marcus frowned. "Are things really that bad?"

Raimond nodded. "I fear so. The latest dispatches suggest we may be forced completely out of the Holy Land within the next couple of years. The kings of Europe, and the populace, no longer have a desire to send precious resources to fight, and now seem content to let the unholy Saracen scourge take it. Hopefully someday we shall return, but I fear it won't be in my lifetime."

Marcus felt queasy at the thought. The Holy Land lost, abandoned by Christendom to the infidel Muslims. It was almost a blasphemous thought, but there was no denying the Crusaders were losing with their dwindling numbers and some idiotic campaigns like that of Hattin. It was only a matter of time before the entirety of the Holy Land was overrun and lost.

A few months ago, he would have happily died in the fight to prevent that, yet sitting here, today, his priorities had changed. Back then, he had nothing to live for but the Order and his duty to God. Today he had two small children, totally reliant on him.

A task he was woefully ill-prepared for, and one that terrified him more than any horde of Saracens.

Lost in thought, he nearly flinched when he noticed Raimond staring at him with a slight smile.

"You're wondering if you're up to the task."

"Sir?"

"Of remaining here, in this land that was once your home, to raise two small children."

Marcus nodded. "Yes, I must confess I have my doubts." He tilted his head toward Simon. "I also fear I have asked too much of my men."

"It was our choice, sir."

"Yes, I know, but if I asked if you would join me cleaning latrines for the rest of our days, you and the others would happily say yes."

"This is true. But eventually, you'd figure out we weren't sincere when yet another shovelful of excrement filled your face by accident."

Marcus chuckled then stared at him, serious. "Are you truly willing to sacrifice your future and remain here?" He raised a finger before Simon could reply. "The truth. There is no shame or repercussions for giving me an answer you think I might not like."

Simon turned in his chair, staring directly into his eyes. "Sir, what you call a sacrifice, I call a challenge. We have done more than our fair share of battle in the name of the Lord. Now two of His children need our help, and I am honored to do my part in His bidding. Never fear that I made a choice that I'm not happy with, and won't be happy with. My place is at your side, and if I felt what you were doing wasn't worthy of a Templar Knight, then my place would no longer be where it is today. Whatever decision you make, know that you have my support, and that of Jeremy and David."

Marcus smiled slightly, then reached out and patted his friend on the shoulder. "You're a fool, and a good friend. I think we shall make a good team, you and I."

"Agreed. But let's try to use the animals for that. I have no desire to be a beast of burden dragging a plow through the soil."

Marcus and Raimond roared with laughter, not noticing the messenger standing in the doorway.

Raimond raised a hand. "Yes, what is it?"

"A message from headquarters, sir."

"Let's see it."

The young man hurried forward, presenting the document with both hands and a bow. Raimond took it and quickly scanned what was written, a frown creasing his face. "Well, gentlemen, we've found out where our brothers and friends are being held."

Marcus leaned forward. "Where?"

"Montry. Apparently once all have arrived, they will be taken to Paris."

Marcus stood, the others following. "This could be good. It provides us with a delay. I suggest I go there at once with David."

Simon's eyebrows rose slightly. "And am I to shovel latrines?"

"Yes, but first I want you to go to Paris and get the original documents provided by the forger's son. I think we will need them to prove our brothers' innocence."

Raimond nodded. "A good plan." He motioned to

the messenger. "Wait here. I want you to go with the sergeant to Paris with a letter from me confirming his orders." He smiled at Simon. "And you are not familiar with all the shortcuts our messengers use to cut down on travel time." The smile disappeared. "For I fear if we are not swift, we will be too late."

Durant Residence
Paris, Kingdom of France

Thomas Durant sat in his father's shop, a steady stream of neighbors and friends having stopped by, once word had spread of the goings-on. Many were here to express their sincere condolences, though he suspected most merely wanted to lay eyes upon the scene of the crime, and question him about the lurid details.

It disgusted him.

But it did distract him.

His stomach growled, and he was finally forced to acknowledge the food that now occupied his father's workplace. The more sincere had often brought some small token for him—bread, cheese, some sausage. These were poor people, but they understood charity, and probably understood his need more than he did at this moment.

He was alone.

His parents were dead, he had no surviving brothers or sisters, his only sibling, a sister, dead before she reached the age of two. It had been so long ago, he sometimes forgot she existed. His grandparents had died long ago, and if he had any aunts and uncles, he didn't know them, his father having moved them twenty years ago from the ancestral lands to the city of opportunities Paris represented.

He wondered if things had worked out the way his father had thought they would. He *had* stayed in business for over twenty years. That had to count for something. They had been hungry at times, though nothing compared to some of the people he had seen begging in the streets. But they always had a roof over their heads—sometimes leaky—and always had clothes on their back—too often patched.

It had been a reasonable life. Nothing like Bernard's, he was sure, though better than many.

And now it was over.

He was alone.

He broke off a piece of cheese and chewed, pouring a cup of wine from a bottle left earlier. They both tasted good. He suddenly realized how hungry he was, having not eaten since the night before. He devoured bits of everything in front of him, until finally he sat back, stuffed to his ears, a satisfied smile on his face.

Then he saw the bloodstain on the floor, and raced to the back and into the alley to retch it all up. He filled a bucket of water and dumped it on his mess, then filled it again and returned to the office, pouring it over the floor where his father had bled out, rinsing away the last remnants through the floorboards.

Then dropped into a corner and cried, staring at the spot as the wood slowly dried, eventually falling asleep, exhausted.

A knock at the door woke him, and he was about to scramble to his feet when he decided better of it. He just wanted to be left alone. The light from outside was now dim, much of the day apparently slept away. His body ached, his stomach demanded attention, and his mouth was sticky with thirst.

And his head pounded from too much wine.

Another knock, this time a little more forceful.

It enraged him.

"Go away!"

"My name is Simon Chastain. I am a sergeant of the Knights Templar. I am seeking Mr. Thomas Durant."

Thomas' eyes widened, and this time he did scramble to his feet, wiping his stained cheeks with the back of his hands, and brushing off his clothes. He stepped forward and opened the door, an imposing figure of a man in black surcoat with red cross filling the doorframe.

"Are you Thomas Durant?"

"Y-yes, sir." He stepped aside. "Please come in."

Simon stepped inside and surveyed the state of the small shop. "I heard about your father. You have my condolences."

"Th-thank you, sir."

Simon produced two documents, opening them slightly for Thomas to see. "You recognize these?"

Thomas nodded. "My father wrote them."

"Exactly. And this has caused quite the problem for quite the number of people."

"I-I apologize. I don't think he wanted to. I mean, I'm sure he didn't, but one doesn't say 'no' to nobility."

Simon grunted. "No, one typically doesn't."

Thomas' stomach grumbled, and he stared at the floor sheepishly.

Simon chuckled, gesturing toward all the food. "You have so much food here, yet sound hungry."

Thomas stared at the floor. "I-I ate, but got sick."

Simon placed a hand on Thomas' shoulder, gently pushing him toward his father's chair. "Sit, and eat. I have something to ask of you, and should you accept, you will need a full belly."

Thomas nodded then sat, wondering what a Templar sergeant could possibly want from him. Simon sat on the opposite side of the table, eying the food, and it occurred to him that his guest might be hungry as well. He waved a hand at the selection. "Please, join me."

Simon smiled. "Thank you, it's been a demanding journey." He attacked the food, and the delight he took in it ignited Thomas' own desire to join in—if he didn't, at the rate the huge warrior was eating, there might be nothing left for him should he delay. As they continued to eat, Simon's pace slowed, then finally he sat back in his chair, patting his stomach. "I thank you, though I think my horse will curse you for increasing her load."

Thomas smiled, the first smile of the day. "You're welcome."

"Now, let me tell you why I am here."

Thomas swallowed and pushed from the desk. "Please."

"You might not be aware, but this document your father created is being treated as genuine. All of the men who are to have signed it, along with any Templars in their company, are being arrested as we speak. They are being charged with treason against the King, and will be taken to Paris, likely tomorrow morning. If they reach there, and the King is presented with this forgery, they will no doubt be executed, and a decree issued for the arrest of all

Templars within the kingdom."

Thomas gulped, feeling sick again. "I-I'm so sorry."

"There is no need for you to apologize. Your father obviously realized the danger of what he was forced to create, otherwise he never would have written this confession. *This* confession, so cleverly executed by your father, could save countless lives. His inclusion of the forged signatures at the bottom of it, proving that it was his hand that had created the original forgery, should be enough to clear the names of those involved."

Thomas didn't feel nauseous anymore, instead, a surge of pride in his father pushing away the melancholy. He said nothing, instead waiting for Simon to tell him how he could possibly help in this untenable situation.

"I have been tasked to bring these documents to where those arrested are being gathered before being taken to Paris, so that we can try to prevent this from ever reaching the King's court."

Thomas couldn't wait any longer. "How can I possibly help?"

"You are the only witness. You saw Sir Bernard here, you drank with him, he confessed his plan to you, then you saw him leaving with your father dying on this very floor. *You* will lend even more credence to these documents' authenticity."

Thomas' heart slammed hard, and his forehead beaded with sweat. "Y-you want me to go with you?"

Simon nodded firmly. "Yes. I want you to accompany me, and together we will save the lives of these innocent men, and the Order I have sworn to protect. Will you help me in this noble deed?"

Thomas gulped, his mouth suddenly dry. He grabbed a cup and took a large drink, slamming it back on the desk a little harder than he had intended, the contents sloshing over the sides and onto the scarred wood. He sucked in a deep breath, steadying himself before staring directly into the eyes of the proud warrior sharing his food. "I consider it my duty to right the wrongs committed by my father, and an honor to assist the Templars in their time of need."

Simon smiled, then rose from his chair and extended a hand. Thomas stood and shook it, the grip as firm as any he had experienced. "You are a brave man, Mr. Durant, and it is an honor to be in your presence." He let go of Thomas' hand then stepped back from the table. "I have two horses for us outside, fully provisioned, and a guide. If there is anything you need, get it now, for we leave at once."

Montry, Kingdom of France

"Look at that! The spectacle! It's completely uncalled for!"

Sir Marcus agreed with David's assessment of what they saw before them. Almost a dozen men were held in the center of the town, chained together, given no place to rest. Instead, those too exhausted from their ordeal, were forced to sit in the mud, much to the delight of the King's Personal Guard surrounding them, and the townsfolk who encircled the prisoners, hurling rotting food and insults at those worse off than them.

It enraged him.

Proud tunics of the Templars were soiled with mud and stained with decaying vegetables, their owners trying to maintain their dignity, their heads held high, even if forced to sit in the dirt, their old bones too tired to carry them any longer.

He wanted to charge forward into their midst and slice open the bellies of every single person responsible for this.

Yet that would be foolhardy, and merely condemn him to death.

But being here, now, he had no idea what he could do to stop this. Simon should be in Paris by now, with the documents in hand to prove their innocence, yet he wouldn't be here until morning. They were but two, he and David, and even if they weren't, attacking in force would merely cause more problems, perhaps convincing the King that they were indeed guilty.

No, they had to be patient. They needed to wait for Simon, then put a stop to this.

But how?

If those holding the prisoners knew about the forgery, then they wouldn't care about the evidence Simon was bringing. He had to assume among them were the murderers posing as Templars, which meant they had no honor, and no interest in the truth. Sir Bernard was probably one of those he was staring at right now, a cluster of knights not a hundred paces from their vantage point.

If Simon arrived before these men departed, they might be merely delivering the proof of these men's guilt into their hands, so they could destroy it, thus condemning everyone here, and the entire Templar Order, to death.

His heart ached with the thought, and his shoulders tensed with the frustration.

He didn't know what to do.

Though he did know what *not* to do.

This was not the place to bring this travesty to an end. It would have to be somewhere else, where someone who outranked these men would be involved, where someone with some honor, and an interest in the truth, could be presented with the evidence of the true crimes committed here, and be convinced to bring an end to this.

Which meant they would have to follow these men to wherever they were going, and hope for an opportunity to intercede on behalf of these innocent prisoners.

"Now what are you two up to?"

Marcus spun toward the voice behind them,

cursing himself for not having paid more attention. It was a rookie mistake, though he had planned for this very possibility, having left their armor, weapons, and anything that might identify them as Templars, outside of town—except for their tunics, the only ones they had. They had turned them inside out, and purposefully soiled them to disguise the cross which had still been slightly visible. He had to hope it was enough.

Marcus smiled at the two foot soldiers now facing them. "Just watching the show."

"If you're so interested, then why not join the crowd?" They both stepped forward and shoved them from the alley and into the dusk and torchlight. "Can you see these traitors better now?"

Marcus nodded, resisting the urge to tear their throats out. "Yes, sir, yes we can. Thank you, sir." He had never cowered in his life, but it was best now to make as the meek peasant he was pretending to be, David thankfully making a good show of it as well.

The two soldiers laughed, then walked off, Marcus repeatedly bowing low as he breathed a sigh of relief. He made to approach the crowd, to join in for a few moments before making their way out of town, when a commanding voice cut through the jeers.

"Bring those two here, now!"

En route to Montry, Kingdom of France

Simon glanced over his shoulder at young Thomas, his eyes wide with fear as they raced down the path in the failing light. Night riding was always more dangerous, but there was a trick to it that too many novices weren't aware of.

Horses were far more attuned to the risks underfoot than their riders.

"Ease up on the reins!" he yelled. "Let the horse guide you!"

Thomas nodded, complying, and when his ride continued without his constant interference, he visibly relaxed. They would cover as much distance as they could before they would be forced to stop, a new moon an unhappy occurrence tonight that would prevent them from continuing. Though it was unfortunate timing, he doubted those responsible for the injustices of the past few days would risk nighttime travel in such conditions either, and would feel no need to do so, regardless.

As far as they were concerned, they were getting away with their crimes.

The fact young Thomas remained unmolested, suggested they felt no sense of urgency in eliminating him as a witness. After all, Simon had found the young man in his own home. If Sir Bernard or his cohorts were concerned about this loose end, surely they would have sent someone to kill him before he could talk.

Simon's eyes narrowed as they crossed a covered

201

bridge. Why hadn't they tried to kill Thomas? He could understand Bernard not doing it, since he was probably in a hurry to deliver the forgery to his partners, but surely someone would have been sent back to eliminate the only other person who knew of their crime. According to Thomas, Bernard had confessed the entire plan to him, and if Thomas remembered, surely Bernard did as well.

He sat upright as a thought occurred to him, his horse slowing automatically.

Nobody else knows!

If nobody else knew about the forgery, then only Bernard would know Thomas needed to be eliminated, and only he could do it without raising suspicions. He couldn't simply order some of his men to travel to Paris, seek out the son of a known forger, and have him killed for no reason. At least not without raising suspicions.

But if the others were in on his plans, then there would be no shortage of those who could come and clean up the mess left behind.

The fact they hadn't, had to mean that Bernard was acting alone, which would match Thomas' story. Bernard had concocted this plan all by himself, and hadn't told anyone, in order to appear the hero.

That had to be it. There could be no other explanation that Simon could think of. Thomas was alive because Bernard was the only one who knew he needed to die, and didn't have time to take care of it, because he was the only one who knew of the forgery, and was determined to be present when the incriminating evidence was presented to a grateful King, who had never held love in his heart for the

Knights Templar.

He glanced back at Thomas, the young man more settled in his saddle now that he realized the horse was better equipped to handle the low light level than his own paltry senses. Simon frowned. Once Bernard was successful in his plot to bring down the Templars with his forgery, he would come for Thomas to eliminate any chance of his crime being discovered.

And with the Templars like himself arrested, and perhaps executed, there would be no one to protect the young man.

His jaw squared and he faced forward once again, damning the timing as the last slivers of light faded and their guide slowed to a halt.

They were done for the day, and he just prayed that his enemy did as expected, and stayed put until the morning, otherwise there might be no hope of intercepting them before they reached Paris.

And the King.

Montry, Kingdom of France

Sir Valentin stared at the two men as they were brought before him. They looked familiar, and that shouldn't be. Not in these parts. He had never spent any time here, and any townsfolk should be complete strangers to him.

Yet these two, especially the older one, seemed familiar. They were dressed unremarkably, their clothes soiled though not in tatters, the cloth appearing cheap, their shoes and leggings functional though of poor quality. They appeared to be peasants in all manner except bearing.

It was their cowering in fear at the abuse by his men that had made him take notice. They didn't seem genuinely scared. He had seen enough plays to know when someone was acting, and these two were acting. Badly. There was no fear in their hearts, no terror in their eyes.

These men were not whom they pretended to be.

"What is your name?"

"Jean," replied the older man. "This is my brother, Paul." He stared at Valentin, raising his hands toward him, his face doing a fairly decent imitation of someone pleading for forgiveness. "Sir, we've done nothing wrong. We merely wanted to see what was happening. We were on our way home when you had us brought before you."

Valentin stared at him, now certain he had encountered these men before. Even the voice seemed familiar. "Have we met before?"

"Jean" lowered his eyes toward the ground as his head shook vigorously. "Surely not. I don't know if I've ever had the honor of meeting a knight, sir."

Valentin grabbed the man by the chin and forced him to look up. He stepped closer, staring into the man's eyes, finding not even a hint of fear there. "You are *not* a peasant."

"I am a farmer, like my brother."

"Where is your farm?"

"Just outside of town."

And then it occurred to him where he had met this man and his companion before. He stepped back, a smile slowly spreading. "The tavern in Crécy-la-Chapelle."

The man's eyes narrowed, and his companion's face expressed the first truly genuine emotion yet.

Resignation.

"I'm not sure what you're talking about."

"You were the drunk at the tavern, who challenged me and my men to a fight."

"I'm sure you have me mistaken for someone else."

Valentin drew his sword, pointing it at the man's chest. "You're a Templar Knight!"

Swords were drawn all around the men, the two imposters quickly encircled as the man's cowering form slowly straightened into the proud warrior he actually was. He lifted his tunic over his head then turned it inside out, revealing the bright red cross that marked the traitorous order, his companion doing the same, his tunic a brown instead of white.

"Your name?"

"I am Sir Marcus de Rancourt, Templar Knight. This is my squire, David. I ask that he be let go, as he has no involvement in this beyond obeying my orders."

"He has sworn an oath to an Order that we now have proof plots against the King. His station within your traitorous organization is irrelevant."

Marcus frowned, glancing about as if searching for someone. "All is not what it seems, Sir…?"

"Valentin de Vaux."

Marcus bowed slightly, Valentin returning the gesture, courtesy among knights universal, even if the enemy. "I thought perhaps I had the honor of addressing Sir Bernard de Claret."

Valentin eyed him. Why would this man think that? Why would he even know of Bernard? He glanced over his shoulder and saw Bernard amidst a group of his men about fifty paces away, no doubt recounting his heroic deeds that had changed the men's opinions of him dramatically.

It had even changed his own.

To face down a member of the aristocracy alone, to interrogate him successfully, to intimidate him enough into not only admitting the document they sought existed, but to produce it as well, he would have thought was impossible if asked yesterday. Yet here they stood, the document in hand, the accused all either dead or in chains in this very town square, over a dozen of their Templar accomplices in custody, all because the most cowardly, inept man he knew, had miraculously faced down what should have been his superior foe in every way, and won.

If he didn't have the document on his person, he

never would have believed it possible.

And now this Templar Knight, someone he had encountered only a few days ago at a tavern in the town of their first victims, was asking of him. Could word have already spread of his deeds, and the Templars were looking to kill him in revenge?

That was possible. Bernard had been boasting every chance he got, and he was sure tongues were wagging among the men and those they encountered. It was conceivable these Templars had been sent to kill him, perhaps even to retrieve the document proving their treasonous plot.

He smiled at the knight. "You would have me identify him, so that you may know the face of the man who is your undoing? So that you can point him out to your accomplices hidden among the crowd, so that they may seek their revenge upon him? What sort of fool do you think I am?"

Marcus stared at him, his face as serious as any Valentin had ever regarded. "You, sir, I am confident, are no fool. But you are being played for one."

Valentin regarded him. "And what is that supposed to mean?"

Marcus frowned. "Unfortunately, now is not the time to explain. But in time, you will understand that what is happening here, today, is an injustice, and you are but a pawn in a clever puppet master's magnum opus."

An ember of anger sparked in Valentin's belly, and he was tempted to end this man's life right then, but he held back. There was something in his words that made him stop, an inner voice telling him to let this man live, as he might yet prove useful, though in a way he couldn't yet fathom.

He stepped back, sheathing his sword. "Put them with the others."

"Sir, the transports are here!"

Valentin glanced over his shoulder to see half a dozen wagons approaching, and he smiled. "Excellent. Load the prisoners immediately. We leave tonight."

Montry, Kingdom of France

Simon waited outside the town of Montry, his patience growing thin as he and Thomas concealed themselves in the forest, awaiting the return of their guide. He had been gone almost an hour, and Simon was becoming concerned the young man might have been arrested.

He stared at his surcoat, wondering if displaying the Templar colors was wise, considering what was going on. Part of him refused to give in to the lies, convinced that removing the symbols of his Order would be showing cowardice, though the more logical part of him countered with the fact that at this moment in time, he might be the only hope to save the Order. He had the sole witness to the crime, and the proof of it in his saddlebags.

"Someone's coming!" hissed Thomas, cowering behind his horse. Simon placed his hand on the pommel of his sword, then breathed easy as he spotted their guide, Mario, picking his way through the trees.

"Over here."

Mario flinched, then visibly relaxed as he pressed through the brush. Simon regarded him and frowned, the young man clearly not bearing good news.

"What did you find out?"

Mario took a water flask offered him by Thomas. "I'm afraid it's not good." He took several large gulps, then handed the flask back. "Sir Valentin and his men left for Paris with the prisoners last night."

Simon muttered a curse, smacking a fist into his other palm. "We should have traveled through the night."

Mario shook his head. "It would not have mattered. They would have been hours ahead of us."

"What of Sir Marcus? Did you see him?"

Mario sighed. "I fear this is the worst news. The reason we didn't find him and his squire at the rendezvous point, is that they were recognized and arrested just before the departure for Paris."

"Recognized? By whom?"

"By Sir Valentin himself. Apparently, there was some altercation at a tavern?"

Simon's jaw dropped as the connections were made. Valentin must have been one of the three knights Marcus confronted while drunk. Marcus wouldn't have remembered them, therefore wouldn't have thought keeping his distance would be necessary. The members of the King's Personal Guard were sober, however, and would have easily recognized the man, a Templar Knight, that had accosted them only a few nights before.

Damn the drink!

"Were they harmed?"

Mario shook his head. "My contact said calm words were exchanged, your master conducting himself quite bravely. They were arrested and transported with the others. I have no information to suggest they were harmed. At least here."

Simon frowned at the addition. He had little doubt that if Marcus and David made it out of the town alive, they would remain that way until they reached their destination, where they would likely be put on trial, then executed.

And the Order would be finished.

"Why were you gone so long?"

Mario smiled slightly. "Because I encountered another one of our messengers."

Simon eyed him. "You have a smile. I sense good news?"

"Perhaps. He was carrying a message from the delegation from Rome."

Hope swelled through Simon's body at the mention of the Papal delegation sent from Rome to meet with King Philip and the Templars from the Holy Land. "Yes? What did he say?"

"They are here! Not even an hour ahead of us, on their way to Paris."

Suddenly trepidation filled him as he recalled the Pope's representatives were to be accompanied by Templars for protection. "Do they know what is going on?"

Mario shook his head. "As far as I know, they are completely unaware."

Simon closed his eyes, cursing once again. "Then they are heading into a possible trap."

Mario nodded. "Perhaps. But apparently they are over two-hundred strong."

Simon's eyebrows rose as an idea slowly evolved. "We need to intercept them. Now, before they reach Paris!"

Approaching Paris, Kingdom of France

"Why didn't you tell them what was going on?"

Sir Marcus glanced at David, sitting beside him in the cramped transport as it jostled its way to Paris. They were already on the outskirts, and he had little doubt they would reach their destination within the hour. What he didn't know was whether that would be some prison, to await trial, or the royal court, to be presented to the King himself.

He was betting on the latter, which could be fortunate if they had what they needed to prove this entire situation was the creation of one man hell-bent on earning his name. Surely the King would want the truth, and even if he didn't, if he were a co-conspirator, the public revelation that the evidence used to bring down the Templars was fake, would certainly halt any nefarious schemes he might have.

For though the King might be the king, that could change if he lost the support of the nobility that made him so.

And the Templars were powerful, with many friends and allies, not to mention incredible wealth.

Taking them down, on demonstrably false evidence, could prove too difficult to risk.

But all of that was moot if the evidence never arrived, and at this moment, he had no idea where Simon was. Had he made it to Paris? Did he have the copy of the forgery and the confession? He cursed himself for not thinking to tell Simon to bring the forger's son with him. He could prove a valuable witness. Though perhaps all was not lost on that front, the boy living in Paris. If word could get out, someone from the Order could collect the boy and bring him to the court to testify, perhaps in as little as an hour or two.

If he could be found.

"Sir?"

Marcus realized he had been staring through David, his question forgotten. "Sorry. What was your question?"

"Why didn't you tell them what was going on?"

"To what end? We have no proof beyond our word, and these men have already proven they are willing to murder to get what they want." Marcus shook his head. "No, revealing what we know before we have the proof in hand, is too risky."

"But you practically told him that you knew something he didn't."

Marcus nodded. "Yes. As a test."

"A test?"

"Yes. I wanted to see how he would react. If he knew what I was talking about, I think his reaction would have been somewhat different, don't you?"

David shrugged. "I'm really not sure. I suppose."

"Well, think about it. If you knew everything was based on a lie, and someone suggested to you that they knew the truth, then what would you do? I can think of several possibilities. One would be that he might kill me on the spot so I could tell no one what I knew. Another might be to mock me, to suggest that no matter what I thought I knew, there was nothing I could do about it, perhaps because he truly felt that way, or perhaps to make me think whatever I knew was of no importance."

"But he did neither."

"Exactly. Which makes me think Sir Valentin may have no idea what is actually going on here."

"Yet he is still a murderer."

"I think we can be certain of that. If he was indeed one of the three we encountered at the tavern, then it is clear to me that those three men were there to commit the first of the murders, and are the three imposters we have been seeking."

"I think you're right. But who will believe us?"

"Probably no one. We need that forgery presented to our ultimate accuser, the King, and for the forger's confession to be believed."

David's eyes shot wide. "Do you think that's even possible? I mean, an audience with the King?"

"We all know the King is not a fan of the Templars. Nobody likes those they owe money to. And we know the King's Personal Guard go nowhere without his personal approval. This mission was done at his behest, and now that everyone believes it has borne fruit, these men will want to present the proof to him in person, and he will want to receive it in front of his court to show he had been right all along to fear the motives of our Order, and by extension, Rome's."

David grasped at his temples. "It's just so much to fathom. A delegation from the Holy Land murdered, a king trying to destroy the Order and by extension, the Church. Forgeries, lies, murder, deceit. I cannot believe we have found so much sin in our homeland. I had always thought coming home would mean an end to all of that which we lived with daily in the Holy Land."

Marcus smiled slightly. "I too was mistaken on that front, but when this is all over, and should we survive, I say we carve out our own little part of this kingdom, and seek the peace that has escaped us our entire lives."

David smiled broadly. "That sounds good to me." He paused. "With my own room?"

Marcus chuckled. "My friend, if we survive the day, then everyone shall have their own room."

"We're here!" shouted someone ahead, and everyone in their transport turned to look down the road, and any joviality that might have been present was wiped away with the view ahead of them.

The Palais de la Cité.

Home of King Philip IV, the King of France.

And no friend of the Templars.

En route to Paris, Kingdom of France

Simon leaned forward in his saddle, urging his horse on at breakneck speed as he followed their guide, Thomas taking up the rear. He checked over his shoulder, the young man immediately behind him, determination on his face, rather than the fear of the night before.

He sensed the urgency as well. If they didn't warn the Papal delegation about to arrive in the city, depending on the state of affairs when they reached their destination, they could be met with overwhelming force and arrested. It all depended on when they arrived.

And how.

They had to beat Sir Bernard and his co-conspirators, though he feared there was little chance of that. But if they could reach the palace in time, perhaps they could beat the issuance of any decrees that might order the arrest of all Templars across the kingdom.

An order Simon had no doubt would spread across all of Christendom, for if the Templars were willing to work toward overthrowing one king, then why not another? Or them all?

"I see them!" shouted Mario over his shoulder.

Simon rose slightly in his saddle and spotted the rear of the convoy, Templar and Papal flags clearly visible.

And a rearguard already turning to challenge them.

"Ease up!" ordered Simon, slowing his steed,

Mario doing the same a moment later. Simon took the lead, his sergeant's surcoat enough to put at ease the knights now challenging them.

"State your business!"

"I need to speak to your commander. I have urgent news."

The knight assessed him for a moment, then nodded. "Follow me." The knights surrounded Mario and Thomas, as Simon was led to the center of the still advancing procession, a distinguished knight, his long gray beard a vibrant white, examining the new arrival.

"Sir, he says he has urgent news."

The knight motioned for Simon to ride beside him. "Your name, sergeant?"

"Simon Chastain, under the command of Sir Marcus de Rancourt."

The knight's eyes widened. "Sir Marcus? I know him well. I am Sir Jermaine de Gardannes. We served together for many years. How is he?"

Simon shook his head. "He's been arrested, sir. That's what I've come to warn you about. You may be heading into a trap."

Sir Jermaine raised a fist. "Halt!" The order was repeated up and down the convoy, and he turned his horse to face Simon. "Explain."

"Sir, there have been several murders, committed we believe by members of the King's Personal Guard. Sir Marcus was investigating these crimes at the behest of Sir Raimond de Comps, and the local Bailiff's Delegate. These murderers disguised themselves as Templars"—this elicited raised eyebrows from Jermaine and muttered utterances from those now surrounding them—"and have been seeking a

217

document that they believed implicated our Order in a conspiracy to overthrow the King."

"Preposterous!"

"I agree, sir, and we now have the proof that it is indeed so." He produced the copy of the forgery, and the signed confession, handing them to Jermaine, then turned in his saddle toward the rear of the convoy. "Please have the boy brought forward!" The order was passed along, and he returned his attention to Jermaine as he read the documents, his cheeks reddening with anger. "I have the forger's son with me. Sir Bernard told him everything over too much drink, and was with his father in his dying moments."

"He was killed?"

"Yes, by Sir Bernard."

"You're certain of this?"

"Yes. The son saw Sir Bernard leave only moments before he discovered his father bleeding to death, and his father told him so. There can be no doubt."

Jermaine's head slowly bobbed. He shook the papers. "This is most disturbing. You say this Sir Bernard is behind it. I'm not familiar with him. What can you tell me?"

"All that I've been able to gather is that he is not very well respected, though his family is. Thomas here"—he gestured toward Thomas as his companions arrived—"would be able to tell you more, but there is no time. Sir Bernard has concocted this plan to try and gain respect in the court. We don't even know if anyone else knows about the forgery. He could be passing it off as the genuine article. It was Sir Marcus' hope that by revealing it to be a forgery, this entire affair could be forgotten. But in order to do that, we must intercept the King's Personal Guard escorting the arrested men named on that document before they reach the King."

Jermaine pursed his lips. "You said Sir Marcus has been arrested?"

"Yes, along with one of his squires, David. Many Templars were apparently arrested along with those named in the forgery, and are being taken to Paris."

"When did they leave?"

"They left from a town less than an hour from here late last night."

Jermaine shook his head. "Then they are most likely already at their destination."

Simon frowned. "Agreed, though perhaps not long enough to have done much damage, as they were traveling with wagons."

"Yes, but enough has probably been said already to prevent us from seeking an audience with His Majesty."

"Well, I had a thought about that."

Jermaine's eyebrows rose slightly. "And that thought was?"

"We don't *seek* an audience."

A smile slowly spread across Jermaine's face. "You propose to not give the King a choice?"

Simon shrugged. "If we are to be condemned as traitors, what more could he do to us?"

Jermaine tossed his head back and laughed, the others gathered joining in. "I like the way you think, sergeant." He rose in his saddle. "Leave ten to guard the dignitaries. The rest, to the palace with haste!"

Palais de la Cité
Paris, Kingdom of France

Sir Marcus shuffled toward the rear of the transport, leaping to the ground when it was finally his turn. He stared in awe at the spectacle, the palace a sight to behold, the only thing comparable in his mind, Saint Peter's Basilica in Rome, something he had only seen once on his way to the Holy Land twenty years ago.

There were sights more beautiful in the Holy Land, but they were usually ancient and well worn, scarred by battle and the elements, their beauty coming from the history within their walls, and the knowledge of the souls who had once walked the spaces contained within.

And though the history here wasn't something he felt any connection to, it was still an impressive sight, and by the reception they had received already, it was clear they were expected, and that whatever was to happen here would happen expediently. There had been no stop at a prison beforehand, no attempt to interrogate anyone. This wasn't to be a trial, this was to be a presentation of the guilty, and the evidence to prove it—a forged document, that no one beyond him, David, and Sir Bernard, apparently knew was so.

And without the proof of that forgery, he was at a loss as to what to do. All he could do was pray that somehow Simon reached them in time with the documents, but looking about at the scores of guards, he doubted his sergeant would be allowed past the gates to present the proof of their innocence.

He feared their salvation would never be given the chance to be heard before the decrees were issued dictating their executions and the arrests of all Templars within the kingdom. And once issued, there would be no going back on them, even if the evidence were later presented.

It would be too much of an embarrassment for the King to admit he had been deceived.

As he shuffled toward the grand entrance with the others, their wrists and ankles chained, he stared up at the sky and said a prayer for those with him about to be condemned, for his Order and its faithful, pious members, and for the two small children about to once again lose the hope so recently restored.

His eyes burned and he closed them, a determination growing within that he had to somehow save himself, if only for the sake of the two tiny souls so dependent upon him.

Approaching Paris, Kingdom of France

Simon felt like he once again had a purpose, was once again the warrior monk he had always aspired to be. There was nothing like being surrounded by his brothers to make him feel a part of something larger than himself, to feel that his life had meaning.

And charging on horseback, surrounded by two-hundred knights in full armor and regalia, the white surcoats of the knights, the black of the sergeants, and the brown of the laymen, made him feel like he was back on the battlefields of the Holy Land, racing into battle against an unholy enemy.

How could he ever give this feeling up?

He had meant it when he said he would stay with Marcus on the farm, yet right now, at this very moment, he had his doubts. The rush he felt in times like these was something that brought him closer to God, an almost rapturous feeling overwhelming his body that was the closest thing to eternal bliss he could imagine, and it was how he pictured Heaven would be like for eternity.

Constant ecstasy, surrounded by one's brothers.

As the outskirts of Paris neared, he frowned as they charged past humble farms, tended by peasants forced into a life of eternal poverty, never having taken the vows as he had, voluntarily. Yet did that mean they were any less close to God than he was? Was he better than them because he had volunteered for a life of poverty? And were their lives any less rewarding? Everything he needed was provided to him by the Order. Clothing, food, drink, lodging. Even his horse and equipment were provided. He wanted for nothing. No, it wasn't a life of luxury by any stretch of the imagination, but it was a good life compared to many he had seen.

So how was he any closer to God than these people, who worked hard day in and day out, tending their fields and flocks? If he were indeed committed to a life of serving his Lord, wouldn't the simple life of a farmer, devoted to helping a man he respected tremendously raise two young children, be a better life than one that some might consider selfish? Was it selfish to want to spend one's days with one's brothers, in relative comfort compared to many, with the occasional thrill of battle? He didn't really think so, but as he passed these farms, he wondered just how pious a life he had chosen compared to these good people on either side of the road upon which they now charged.

The farms gave way to the city, and as they pressed through the streets, the curious citizenry rushing out of their way, he saw what true poverty looked like.

And it made him feel even more uncertain as to the life he had chosen. What sacrifices had he truly made? For these people, life was a constant struggle. All he had done was join a brotherhood that gave him everything he needed, in exchange for his loyalty.

A pit formed in his stomach, a pit of shame, at having second thoughts about staying with his brother, with his friend. All doubt was now removed. He would remain, and it would bring him closer to God, which was all he had ever wanted.

Now he just had to save his friend, and his

brotherhood, so that the dream wasn't lost for all.

Palais de la Cité
Paris, Kingdom of France

Sir Marcus watched as the prisoners were unshackled, the King apparently not a fan of the sound the chains made. There had been debate among some, but Sir Valentin had prevailed as the head of the King's Personal Guard.

The guard with the key stopped in front of Marcus and David. "What about these two? They're Templars, and not old like these others."

Valentin approached Marcus, his eyes assessing him. If things were to go badly, if he had any hope of escape, he needed to be free of these shackles, otherwise he'd be led like a lamb to the slaughter.

Marcus raised his chained hands. "*If* we are guilty of the crimes you say we are, then I am indeed a threat. But I am but one man, unarmed. If I were to try anything, then surely your men are capable of stopping me. And should I try something, then surely it would prove my guilt, and your case, against me. Remove my shackles, and let me prove either your case, or mine."

"That I am being played for the fool."

Marcus bowed slightly. "And we both know you are no fool, though no man is above being played for one. It is the fool who eventually doesn't figure it out, but I am confident you will."

Valentin stared at him for a moment, then flicked his wrist. "Remove his shackles. We wouldn't want to annoy the King with their unholy sound." He walked

225

away as Marcus' chains were removed. He rubbed his wrists and watched as David was freed as well.

"You continue to challenge him," whispered David. "Is that wise?"

"I'm continuing to force him to question what is going on."

"And by not telling him? What do you continue to hope to accomplish?"

"I want his imagination to come up with something. If I told him the document was a forgery, he'd simply dismiss it. But by not telling him, by making him question everything, he may yet figure it out himself."

"Now who's the fool?"

Marcus grinned at David. "Let us pray that it is not I, or no amount of royal ass kissing will get either of us out of this."

Paris, Kingdom of France

Thomas' heart slammed, the rush of excitement and terror at this moment overwhelming. He had never ridden this hard before, and never while surrounded by knights in full armor, their colors boldly displayed for all to see.

As they raced through the streets he had grown up in, he spotted the odd familiar face, and was sure some had even pointed at him, though he truly had no time to take notice. This was a desperate charge, these men forcing their way through the crowded streets, almost oblivious to those occupying the cobblestone, knowing that if they failed, they could all be condemned to death.

These were men with nothing left to lose.

He had never been comfortable with his father's line of work—at least his unofficial line. He was proud of him for knowing how to read and write in a world where those skills were rare among their class, and it was a skill he was thankful his father had passed on to him, no matter how much he had complained at first. None of his friends possessed these skills, and it had been a difficult sell on his father's part to convince him it would be a benefit someday.

He had been right. He enjoyed being able to read and write, and when he returned home, he would attempt to keep his father's business alive, though he feared, without the skills of a forger, something he had tried his hand at and failed miserably, there wouldn't be enough money to keep going.

Though he was now supporting only one.

His heart ached at the thought of how his father had died. He had always imagined it being something peaceful, in his sleep. Never could he have dreamed it would be something so horrific, so terrifying. He was stabbed in the stomach, which meant he would have been facing Bernard, possibly looking into his eyes. He would have seen the face of his killer, peering into a soul consumed by evil, and that image would have haunted his final moments.

Thomas thanked the good Lord his work had been canceled. If it hadn't been for that stroke of misfortune, he would have never had those last few moments with his father. He smiled slightly, glancing up at the heavens above.

The Lord works in mysterious ways.

He had been given a gift by his savior, a gift that gave him not only a few more precious moments with his father, but the answers to the mystery that would have gone unsolved. Who had killed him, and why. And now, with the answers to those questions, he had been given an opportunity to not only seek justice, but prevent the destruction of perhaps the most important order of knights to have ever blessed this earth.

All because by some tiny miracle, he had been cheated out of an honest day's labor.

He glanced at the knights on either side of him, their bright white tunics and crisp red crosses inspiring, and he wondered what life as a Templar might be like. He could never imagine himself as a warrior. He didn't have the temperament for it. Though with his skills in reading and writing, and even basic arithmetic, he might be of service to them in some way.

"On guard!"

He glanced ahead but could see nothing, only hear what was happening. Swords clashed, women screamed, and men cried out. The phalanx of man and beast slowed, if only for a moment, then surged forward once again. Thomas glanced to his left and right to see half a dozen of the King's Guard either dead or tending their wounds, no match for the two hundred strong that had challenged them.

He felt a surge of pride to be associated with such great men, then fear gripped him as he realized that should these knights be condemned, he too would be along with them.

He stared at the black surcoat of Simon ahead of him, wondering if he had made the right choice in coming with him.

Palais de la Cité
Paris, Kingdom of France

They had been forced to their knees in front of their king, they had each been named along with their crimes, and now the evidence was being presented, a single piece of evidence, that named but seven of the men here today, the rest all accused of being accomplices.

"I have never seen this document before!" declared the seventh and final signatory, repeating the oath of the previous six. "I will admit that this does appear to be my signature, but I swear to you and to God, that I never signed this document."

Sir Valentin motioned toward the man as he turned to King Philip. "Again, Your Majesty, the words of a found out man. They deny the contents of the document, yet all admit that their signatures appear genuine. Are we to believe these lies? I say their guilt is clear. These men are traitors, plotting against your God-given mastery over these lands and your subjects. These Templars, and their treasonous partners of the aristocracy, have been plotting to overthrow you, and take power for themselves. I, along with my second-in-command, Sir Bernard de Claret"—he bowed toward a man who returned the gesture, slightly deeper, giving Marcus his first confirmation of who the man behind this criminal enterprise was— "uncovered this plot, a plot you so wisely suspected, and it is with great humility that I submit to you that these men are guilty, and deserve immediate execution. I also suggest, humbly, that an immediate decree be issued, ordering the arrest of all Templars within the realm, and the seizure of all their assets within our borders."

Marcus smiled to himself. *That* was what this was about. The assets. The King owed the Templars a massive amount, an amount he could never hope to repay, as his wars hadn't been going to plan. By declaring the bankers criminals, he could seize their funds, and wipe out his debts with one stroke of the pen.

And Marcus was having nothing to do with it.

"Only if the lone piece of evidence is genuine."

The room turned toward Marcus, still on his knees, his eyes, once staring at the floor, now staring at King Philip, sitting on his ornate throne.

"How dare you address His Majesty!" Bernard surged from his position to the side of the proceedings, his hand reaching for his sword.

"Is the case against these men so weak, that it cannot stand a challenge?"

King Philip raised a hand slightly, Valentin blocking Bernard with an arm. "Let him speak."

Marcus suppressed a sigh of relief, slightly surprised he was being given the opportunity, but with the room filled with the royal court, men and women alike turning red with bated breath, the King could hardly deny him his moment.

For why would he? He would assume the document was genuine, unless he was in on this from the very beginning. And every fiber of his being was telling him that this was not so, that Bernard was the only one who knew the truth.

"If I may?" Marcus stood after a nod from the King. He bowed deeply, there no point in disrespecting the man. "Your Majesty, I have information that is of critical importance to these proceedings, and I ask that you indulge me as I lay out the entire story. It may take a few moments, some of it may even sound irrelevant at first, but you have my word as a Templar Knight, and a man of God, that everything I am about to tell you is of importance, and is the truth as I know it to be."

Another wave of the hand.

Marcus bowed again, quickly trying to piece together what he would say and how he would say it, so that he would be given a chance to relay everything necessary, and also delay things enough that Simon might reach them in time with the proof of what he was about to say.

He stepped forward, putting Valentin out of his line of sight, but remaining far enough away from King Philip so as not to pose a threat. "Your Majesty, three days ago, a man and his wife, an auditor working for you, were murdered in Crécy-la-Chapelle. Mr. Fabron and his wife were murdered by men posing as Templar Knights."

"Posing? All witnesses have identified them as Templars," interrupted Valentin. "What proof do you have that they weren't Templars?"

Marcus bowed slightly to his side, acknowledging Valentin, but not looking at him, instead keeping his eyes focused on the King. "If you will please permit me to finish, all will be explained."

And another wave of the hand.

"Thank you, Your Majesty." He turned enough to

give Valentin a slight look, implying he shouldn't interrupt what the King so obviously wanted to hear. He continued. "Two nights before these murders, myself and three of my men encountered three of your guard in a local tavern. One of them was Sir Valentin." He spun toward the knight. "Do you deny this?"

"I deny nothing."

Marcus bowed, smiling slightly. "Thank you." He returned to the King. "Three men disguised as Templars committed the murders two days later. What they aren't aware of"—he turned toward Valentin—"is that there was a witness to that crime, who saw the faces of two of the murderers, and can identify them."

Valentin appeared to pale slightly, and the court erupted with gasps and muttered surprise. Valentin squared his shoulders. "Then I demand this witness be brought forward!"

An excellent recovery.

Marcus turned back to the King. "Your Majesty, I can produce this witness, though it will take a day, as he is at my farm in Crécy-la-Chapelle. He saw the murder of his parents, and heard the conversation that took place before their deaths. These men were seeking a document, and we must assume it is this very document that has been presented to you, incriminating these men in a treasonous plot against you."

He turned to Valentin. "Without any accusation that you were the one who committed the murder, will you confirm that you have been seeking this document for at least the past several days?"

Valentin appeared uncertain of what to say, glancing at his king, who gave an almost imperceptible nod. "Yes, I can confirm this."

"And why were you seeking it?"

"I had heard that a clandestine meeting had occurred between the Templar delegation from the Holy Land, and several local Templars and members of the aristocracy known to be sympathetic to their cause. In questioning one of those who attended, I was informed of the existence of this treasonous document. I then took it upon myself to find it."

Marcus thanked God for the phrasing. "Then we can assume that His Majesty was not aware of this undertaking, nor any methods you may or may not have employed to find the document."

Valentin paused, apparently realizing he was being given an out to protect his king. The question was would he take it. If the King was involved in the conspiracy, then this was Valentin's chance to protect him from any embarrassment. But if he solidly believed the document was real, then he might choose to include his king in the conspiracy, because in his mind, there was none, and his king would benefit from the success of the mission. But if he had doubts?

"You are correct. His Majesty ordered me to seek the truth, whatever it may be."

Sighs and murmurs filled the court, everyone present realizing that should things go badly in the next few moments, the King had just been removed from the equation, and any scandal would leave him unscathed.

Marcus bowed slightly. "I thank you for your honesty, Sir Valentin. I believe you to be a man of honor, loyal to his king, who has zealously pursued the truth, and in finding it, successfully brought those accused to justice."

Valentin nodded in acknowledgment, though said nothing.

"Now, let me explain what has occurred since those heinous murders, and please note, in case anyone has missed this point, Mr. Fabron, our first victim, is one of the signatories of this document. Another signatory is Sir Gilbert de St. Leger, commander of one of our outposts in Crèvecœur-en-Brie. I was asked to investigate these crimes by the local Bailiff's Delegate, as well as Sir Raimond de Comps, commander of our Commandry in Coulommiers. I immediately set out to meet with Sir Gilbert, as Sir Raimond believed he had been at the meeting held with the delegation from the Holy Land, a delegation, I might add, that was missing at this point." More surprised utterances from the onlookers. "When we arrived the next day in Crèvecœur-en-Brie, we were dismayed to discover that Sir Gilbert had been murdered in his chambers, the last to have seen him, two Templar Knights who had paid him a visit late the night before."

"Again, Templar murderers!" interrupted Bernard, Valentin spinning and glaring at him.

Marcus acknowledged him. "Yes, two men who appeared to be Templars, were last seen with him. It was at this time that we discovered a document in Sir Gilbert's possession, which was an innocent summary of the meeting held the week before, with the same signatures at the bottom as you have seen on the treasonous document. We now suspected that these men were all to be murdered, and messengers were sent out to warn them. But what we didn't know at the time, was that the most dastardly part of this conspiracy, for it was a conspiracy, even if all involved weren't aware that it was, was to take place."

Even the King leaned forward for his next words.

"Someone in this very room took it upon himself to ensure that these men here today were implicated in this most heinous crime, by providing *false* proof of their support in your overthrow, Your Majesty."

The court erupted as those watching the proceedings turned to look at those around them, all wondering whom it could be that Marcus was accusing.

Valentin stepped into his field of view. "You are accusing a loyal subject of His Majesty of a serious crime. We have entertained your musings long enough. Either provide us with proof of your allegations, or be silent, and accept your punishment."

Somebody shouted at the back of the room, panic in their voice. "We're under attack!"

Marcus smiled. "I believe the proof has just arrived."

Approaching Palais de la Cité
Paris, Kingdom of France

Archers on horseback took down the guards rushing to close the mighty gates of the palace, their writhing forms replaced by more trying to finish the task, but it was too late. The first of the Templar Knights forced their way past the gates, their heavy swords held out to their sides, mowing down any who stood in their path, the unprepared and inexperienced force ceremonially guarding the palace quickly breaking the lines and scattering in all directions.

Simon glanced over his shoulder, urging Thomas to stay close, as the large force of Templars continued forward, several dozen taking control of the gate and closing it behind them to prevent any counterattack from having easy access.

Though Simon doubted there would be any chance of that. This would be over quickly, and if they were to win the day, it wouldn't be by force, but by whether the evidence they were about to deliver would be accepted.

As they reached the main entrance to the palace, the massive force of Templar Knights rushed up the steps, most still on horseback, the guards scattering, and the doors thrown open by several of the laymen now on foot.

Simon led the charge through the doors, determined to find Marcus and David, and hopefully put an end to this travesty of justice.

He only prayed he wasn't too late.

237

The sight before him caused his heart to sink. Over a dozen men, some in their Templar tunics, were on their knees at the head of the massive room, the King now on his feet, his Personal Guard surrounding him with swords drawn, and the elite of Paris, dressed unlike anything he had ever beheld, rushing to the sides of the massive room in fear as two dozen soldiers of the Knights Templar surged into the room.

He brought his horse to a halt and leaped from the saddle, relieved to see Marcus standing before the King, a smile on his face, and if he weren't mistaken, a distinct look of relief as well.

The knights dismounted as more surged into the hall, rushing forward and encircling the accused, swords held on the nobles lining the walls, and the Personal Guard now shielding the King.

Marcus held up his hand. "I'd like to welcome these new guests, who at my behest, are delivering the very proof that I have spoken of." He walked over to Simon, shaking his hand and lowering his voice. "*Please* tell me you have it."

Simon smiled, producing the two documents. "And I brought the forger's son."

Marcus grinned, slapping him on the shoulder. "Who's the fool now?"

"Sir?"

Marcus shook his head. "I'll explain later." He turned to face the King. "Your Majesty, in my hand, I have the proof of the true crime committed here today, and once you read what is written, and hear the testimony of this young man, I trust you will agree that the guilt lies not with these men here before you today, but with another in this room, who has taken advantage of the events of the past several days, in order to further his position in this court."

King Philip sat back down, motioning for his guards to lower their weapons. Immediately, all the Templar Knights sheathed their swords, an anticipatory silence spreading through the room.

And the King finally spoke. "And whom do you accuse, Sir Marcus?"

Marcus bowed deeply at being addressed, an admission, however subtle, that his words were being given a fair hearing. He spun toward Sir Bernard, stabbing a finger in the air at him. "Sir Bernard de Claret!"

Bernard nearly soiled himself, his jaw dropping as his heart hammered. He had suspected this moment was coming as soon as Marcus had begun to speak, and all doubt was removed when the Templar Knights had invaded this sovereign chamber.

So he had repeatedly coached himself as to what to do in that moment he was finally accused.

Drop the jaw and appear shocked.

Which he did, he thought, rather well.

"This is an outrage!" he cried, striding forward to face his accuser. "I demand satisfaction!" It was the only thing he could think of to do. Kill the messenger, and perhaps the message might never be received.

Valentin intervened, much to his dismay, blocking him with a hand to the chest. He glared at him, as if he were beginning to believe the story being laid out.

And it terrified him.

"You will keep your place, and your silence."

"But—!"

Valentin pushed him back several paces, then turned toward Marcus. "Continue."

Marcus bowed. He now clearly had an ally, or at least someone willing to give him a chance to finish nailing shut the coffin Bernard now feared was his fate. He searched the aristocracy, desperate for a friendly face, and finally found his mother and father, on the opposite side of the room, and he knew it was all over.

His father was glaring at him, and his mother had already turned her back.

His life was over.

He took a step backward, toward the entrance to the gardens, when several Templar Knights surrounded him, swords drawn and pointed at his chest and back.

Marcus ignored him. "Your Majesty, it is now time to reveal the entire truth, though if you'll permit me one last interruption?"

A flick of the wrist.

Marcus whispered something into the ear of the man who had brought the documents about to be presented, and Bernard watched him hurry through the crowd toward the entrance.

Marcus held up the documents. "This is an exact reproduction of the document before us today." He handed it to Valentin. "Would you concur?"

Valentin examined it, motioning for the original to be brought forward. He held them up, then nodded. "They appear to be the same."

"And the signatures?"

He held them both up to the sunlight pouring in from the garden, then placed the pages back to back, lining up the signatures. He turned back toward the proceedings, apparently satisfied. "They do indeed appear to be exact matches."

"And does that surprise you?"

Valentin's eyes narrowed. "I'm not certain I understand the question."

"When you sign your name, does it always match *exactly*, every time?"

Valentin's head bobbed slightly. "I see what you mean. I would have to answer, no. There are always variations."

Marcus smiled. "Exactly." He turned to the room, slowly spinning to address them. "As I am certain all these distinguished members of the court will agree, though their signature might appear the same every time, there are deviations. There are none in these."

Nods of assent circled the room, murmured agreement with his statement universal. Marcus held up the second document. "This is a confession from the forger who created both of the documents you now have before you. He has confessed to his crime, named the perpetrator as Sir Bernard, and also reproduced the signatures at the bottom of the document, to prove that it was he who forged the original." He handed the second document to Valentin. "Sir, if you would?"

Valentin again compared the signatures, and nodded, shooting a glare at Bernard that made him cringe. "They are *exactly* the same."

"Which I believe will prove that the document is a forgery."

Bernard stepped forward. "Then I too have been betrayed! This document may be a forgery, but I was

241

not aware of it. Sir Everard de Charney confessed to its existence when I interrogated him, and it was he who gave me it. Whoever had the forgery created has betrayed us all."

Valentin shook the second document. "This names *you*, Sir Bernard. Not somebody else, not Sir Everard, but you!"

"Then someone has posed as me in order to defame me, to implicate me in an unthinkable crime. This entire proceeding is outrageous! I demand to be heard!"

Marcus held up a hand, cutting off Valentin from responding. "I agree you should be heard. But perhaps we should first hear from my final witness." He held out his arm toward the throng of Templar Knights. "May I present to His Majesty, Thomas Durant, the son of the forger, the boyhood friend of Sir Bernard, and to whom Sir Bernard confessed his entire plan to while drunk."

Bernard's heart hammered and his ears pounded with rushing blood as he rose up on his toes, trying to spot his old friend, and the sealer of his fate.

He almost cried out in dismay as Thomas emerged from the crowd of knights, his tiny, nearly emaciated frame, making him appear to be a mere boy compared to these soldiers.

And as Thomas stepped forward, Bernard knew it was all over, a quick glance at his father, now leading his mother from the court, confirming that not even his family would stand behind him.

Simon stepped back outside, the sun shining brightly on the stone courtyard, over one hundred Templars, many still on horseback, guarding the gate and walls, prepared for any attack that might come. But with the proceedings inside sounding like they might be taking a turn for the better, if all continued to go well, they might actually be out of here before any help might arrive.

The several score of captured guards and other palace staff, were held nearby, and he quickly strode over to the group. "Who here is Sir Valentin's squire?"

The gathered group looked at each other, nobody admitting to holding the position, and he had no time to waste.

"Step forward now"—he partially drew his sword—"or I stop asking politely."

Somebody yelped, one of the palace guards stepping through the others, a young man held by the scruff of his neck, his feet barely touching the ground, swinging his arms in an attempt to escape what must have been a crushing grip. "I believe this is the one you're looking for." The young man was deposited in a heap in front of Simon.

"Are you Sir Valentin's squire?"

The man said nothing.

Simon reached down and hauled him to his feet. "I'm not here to hurt you, boy, but if you make me ask again, I'll hand you over to him"—he pointed at the most menacing Templar within view—"and he'll make you wish you were never born."

The knight growled, baring his teeth, the young man immediately trembling.

"Y-yes, I'm his squire."

"Your name?"

"Yannick."

"Very well, Yannick. Where are your master's horses?"

Yannick pointed with a shaky finger to the left of the palace.

"Show me."

Yannick quickly headed in the direction he had pointed, Simon following. They rounded the corner, and a large set of impressive stables were revealed, dozens of horses visible, now tended by several Templar squires. Yannick came to a halt just before the horses, still skittish from the ruckus of only moments ago.

"Which are your master's?"

"He had four."

"Show me."

Yannick picked through the horses, finding the first. Simon motioned for one of the Templar squires to hold it, and soon all four were separated from the group.

"Show me the Templar uniforms."

Yannick paled. "I-I don't know—"

Simon placed a hand on the hilt of his sword, and Yannick's eyes bulged. He rushed toward one of the horses, opened its saddlebags, and retrieved a white surcoat and tunic. He brought them to Simon. Simon handed the surcoat to one of the squires, then examined the tunic. He exchanged it for the surcoat, and almost immediately a smile spread. He pointed at the horse. "And this is Sir Valentin's?"

Yannick nodded.

"Prove it."

Yannick pointed at the horse. "This is his family crest."

"And will you swear to your king that this surcoat was in the saddlebags of your master?"

Yannick hesitated.

Simon stepped slightly closer. "You will be required to answer this question in front of the King. Would you lie to him?"

Yannick's head shook furiously. "N-no."

"Then I ask you again. Will you swear to your king that this surcoat was in the saddlebags of your master?"

Yannick's shoulders sank, and his chin dropped to his chest as he stared at the ground. "Yes."

"And you will swear that you have seen him wear this very disguise over the past several days?"

"Yes."

"That is all I need to hear." Simon turned to the squires. "Bring him and the horse, and be quick about it. There's little time."

"Here they come!" shouted someone from the front gate, causing Simon's heart to beat a little more rapidly. He grabbed Yannick by the tunic and raced toward the palace entrance as a large column of the King's Guard approached the gate, a bloody battle about to begin if he didn't put an end to this soon.

Sir Valentin had taken over the questioning, much to Marcus' relief. It was clear now that Valentin realized he had been deceived, and was now looking to shift all guilt to Bernard. He was indeed a victim here as well, but Marcus was convinced that this man, though perhaps a patsy with respect to the forgery, was the man behind the murders of at least four people, five if one counted the man murdered by Bernard himself.

"And how did you know Sir Bernard?"

"We were friends."

There was some laughter from the crowd, and Valentin smiled. "You, a peasant, were friends with someone from one of the most powerful families in the kingdom?"

Thomas stared at his well-worn shoes, his cheeks burning. "When we were children. My father did some work for his father. That was how we met. We used to sneak out of our homes and meet. That was many years ago, however."

"And now you claim that one of the most powerful families in the realm, had business with a peasant shopkeeper like your father?"

"Yes."

"Your father, a known criminal."

"Not known, sir."

"I beg your pardon?"

"He was not a *known* criminal, sir. You never caught him."

Marcus suppressed a laugh, delighting in the hint of a smile curling at the corners of Thomas' mouth as the audience gave in, their laughter mixed with a few cheers.

"And you claim Sir Bernard, a nobleman, had business with your father two nights ago."

"Yes, sir."

"To create this forgery."

"Yes, sir."

"Do you have proof of what you say?"

"Only my father's confession, the fact the signatures match too perfectly, and my own word."

Valentin scoffed. "I'm to take the word of a peasant over the word of a nobleman?"

"You should take the word of an honest man over that of a liar any day, sir."

Several clapped, and Valentin's tone changed abruptly, a smile spreading.

"And you, good sir, would be correct. I should, and I will. It seems clear to me that we have all been deceived by Sir Bernard, and the proof is in this boy's brave words, and his father's own written confession." He spun on Bernard. "Do you admit to your crimes?"

"I admit nothing!"

"So you would continue to shame your family? You would continue this pattern of cowardliness you have become a laughingstock over? You would continue to be the embarrassment to the aristocracy that you have proven yourself to be to this point?"

Bernard's face was as red as a Templar's cross, his fists clenching and unclenching, as he struggled to maintain control.

He lost.

"I am no coward! I am no laughingstock! Would a man such as this be able to devise a plan so cunning, that even a king could be fooled? Would a coward leave his unit, travel to Paris, commission a forgery so perfect that the great Sir Valentin de Vaux was tricked into bringing it to his king? Would a coward then kill the forger, then kill one of those named on the list to provide a plausible explanation as to how he obtained the document? These aren't the actions of a coward! These aren't the actions of an embarrassment! These are the actions of a knight, worthy of his family name, and worthy of his own respect!

"Yes, I admit to everything you accuse me of, because I was doing what needed to be done! The King wanted proof that the Templars were betraying him, and *you* couldn't find it! Well, I did! I had it created, then found it, then presented it. Me! Me the coward! Me the embarrassment! Me the laughingstock!" He jabbed a finger at Valentin. "Well, who's the embarrassment now? Who's the laughingstock now? You! You, that's who! You fell for my scheme, and if you had the balls you claim to have, you never would have let these vermin"—he spat at Marcus and Thomas—"speak. If you had put them in their place, the King would have had what he wanted, instead of being embarrassed by your incompetence!"

Valentin stood silently, allowing the verbal barrage to continue, each spat phrase another shovelful of dirt dug for the future grave of young Bernard. Marcus bit his tongue, almost drawing blood, as he hid his glee. Bernard had just confessed to everything, including the commission of the forgery, the murder of Thomas' father, and deceiving the King.

Marcus glanced at King Philip, who sat unmoving on his throne, listening to the tirade, no emotion revealed, but his red ears suggesting he was furious.

Bernard finally fell silent, his chest heaving, his forehead beaded with sweat, perhaps having said all that he wanted to, or perhaps realizing he had said too much.

Either way, it was Valentin's turn.

"Arrest this man for treason against the King. Hold him outside."

Bernard was grabbed on either side by two of the guards, his sword and dagger removed. He shook off their grip and straightened his tunic. He glared at Valentin, then turned to King Philip and bowed deeply, not saying a word.

The King ignored him.

He walked past the gathered crowds toward the entrance, the men glaring at him, the women hiding behind their fans, their eyes wide and their cheeks flushed, this probably the most thrilling spectacle most had seen outside the playhouses.

Nothing beat the truth for excitement.

Valentin turned toward King Philip and bowed deeply. "Your Majesty, I must take full responsibility for this fiasco. Sir Bernard was under my command, and I should have known what was happening. I apologize for any embarrassment I may have caused you, and I stand ready to receive any punishment you feel is necessary. All I ask is that you spare my men. They had no more idea of what Sir Bernard was up to than I did, but he was not under their command, so they bear no responsibility."

He bowed even deeper.

"Sir."

Marcus turned to see Simon standing behind him with a Templar squire holding the reins of a horse belonging to the King's Guard, one of the palace squires standing beside it. Simon handed him a Templar surcoat, holding up one of the corners.

Marcus smiled.

He turned toward the King as he considered Valentin's plea. There was little doubt the King would pardon him, laying all the blame on Bernard. After all, they had his confession, and everything here today with respect to the arrests and the charges, were all linked to the forged document.

And if that were the only crime, Marcus would have been content to remain silent.

But it wasn't.

And he wasn't.

"Your Majesty, if I may, there is one other thing to consider before you make your decision on whether or not to assign blame to Sir Valentin."

King Philip redirected his gaze, still saying nothing. Marcus bowed slightly. "There is the matter of the murder of the entire delegation of Templars from the Holy Land, the murders of Mr. Fabron and his wife, and at least three other murders that we know of. One from the delegation, and all of the other victims, with the exception of Mrs. Fabron, were named in the forgery. Surely those responsible for these murders must be brought to justice."

King Philip nodded slightly, his eyes flaring, suggesting he wasn't pleased with this turn of events, and doubt now threatened to rule Marcus. Perhaps he should have simply let things lie as they were a moment ago. The murders had been stopped, they knew who the murderers were, and one of them would likely be put to death, so what was there to be gained? God would deliver justice upon the others, so who was he to pursue this?

He glanced at Thomas, his eyes filled with tears, and thought of young Pierre back at his farm.

That's why you're doing this. He deserves justice. All the families deserve justice.

He drew a deep breath, forging onward. "Your Majesty, when the bodies of the delegation from the Holy Land were discovered, they had been stripped of anything that might identify them as Templars, though a mistake was made. Besides the numbers matching the delegation exactly, they also all carried purses with no more than four *deniers* in them, a princely sum for none."

Murmurs of explanation swept the court as those in the know explained to those who didn't, that only Templars would carry so little money on them due to their vows of poverty.

"And as we've discussed earlier, it was men disguised as Templar Knights that committed the murders." He held up over his head the surcoat handed to him by Simon. "Using the very clothes taken from the murdered delegation!"

Gasps broke out.

He stepped closer to Valentin. "Do you recognize this?"

"Should I?"

Marcus smiled at the response. It sounded outwardly calm, innocent, but it was the eyes that were giving away the truth. "It was taken from your own horse." He motioned toward the horse held by the Templar squire. "This is your horse, is it not?" He quickly strode over to the horse and pointed at the crest. "Is this not your crest? It matches that proudly sewn on your tunic."

Valentin turned slightly red. "It is."

Marcus marched back toward Valentin, holding out the surcoat. "Then I ask again, do you recognize this?"

Valentin nodded. "Yes, I do now. We found a stash of Templar equipment several days ago. My men and I collected it, with the intent of returning it to your Order when our mission was complete."

Marcus bowed, turning to the King then those gathered with a smile, the surcoat held up in one hand, his arms outstretched. "A *very* reasonable explanation. Completely plausible, and one I think we all should believe, as after all, Sir Valentin is a man of honor, has admitted to being duped along with the rest of us by the real criminal, Sir Bernard, and has thrown himself on the mercy of our good King."

Nods of agreement encircled the room.

"And I would agree with everything I just said, if it weren't for one thing."

Hushed silence washed over everyone.

He held up the corner of the surcoat. The *torn* corner of the surcoat. "Except for this one, tiny detail." He stepped toward Valentin, holding up the corner. "Do you see this?"

"Of course."

"And what do you see, for those with poor eyesight."

"A surcoat with a torn corner."

"Exactly! A torn corner. Do you know what happened to that corner?" He held up a finger, cutting off Valentin. "When did you say you found this? Four days ago was it?"

"I believe so."

"Come, my good sir, you must know. You're a knight! An honored nobleman! Surely you can remember when you discovered something as significant as a stash of Templar clothing."

"It was four days ago."

"And you're certain of that?"

"Absolutely."

"Excellent. So you had this robe in your possession four days ago." Marcus spun toward the crowd. "And Mr. Fabron and his wife were murdered three days ago, by men wearing Templar robes, as witnessed by their son, and by townsfolk who saw them race out of town on horseback."

"I fail to see what this has to do with me."

Marcus smiled, reaching into his pocket and producing the piece of cloth found gripped in Mr. Fabron's hand. He held it up for the crowd to see. "In Mr. Fabron's hand, I found this piece of cloth, covered in his own blood, obviously torn from whoever had attacked him and his wife." He tossed the surcoat to a startled Valentin, who caught it, his eyes wide. "Hold out the torn corner for me, would you?"

Valentin stared at him for a moment, but complied, and Marcus strode toward him, the piece of cloth held out in front of him in both hands, the two torn sides pointed toward Valentin, then abruptly stopped, bringing the piece into position, revealing a perfect match for the missing corner.

"It matches!"

Gasps and cries exploded around him, shouts of indignation erupting from some as the truth of what had just been revealed was realized.

He held up the piece of cloth. "Direct from the dead man's hand, is the proof of who committed his murder, the murder of his poor, innocent wife, and most likely the murders of several others." He swung an arm out to his side, pointing directly at Valentin, playing his role as if an actor on the stage. "I give you, Your Majesty, your murderer!"

253

Outrage enveloped the room and Valentin went red, his eyes narrowing as he glared at Marcus like a cornered animal. What happened next would seal the man's fate.

He drew his sword, a roar escaping as he did so.

Admission of guilt?

"Sir!"

Marcus spun to see a sword tossed by Simon soaring through the air. He leaped up and grabbed it, swinging to parry the first blow from Valentin. Screams from the ladies gathered wasn't enough to cause the crowds to flee, all too terrified and enthralled with what was happening. Marcus slowly circled with his enemy, the King's Guard at the ready, not to help their disgraced commander, but to protect the King, a king who now leaned forward on his thrown, apparently as eager as his subjects to see blood drawn this day.

And Marcus was happy to oblige, for today he was an instrument of God, sent here, at this moment, to deliver this murderer of innocents to the depths of Hell.

He had been in many sword fights over the decades, and had usually been victorious. But he was old now, probably ten years the senior to Valentin. Yet youth wasn't everything, just as strength wasn't. As a Templar, he had dueled almost every day for twenty years, often against men he would characterize as twice his size, and far too many nearly half his age.

Which meant fear didn't rule his heart, nor did anger. His thoughts were pure. He was an instrument of good, and he recognized in his foe not only fear, but anger.

Two emotions that had no place in a battle one hoped to win.

Valentin swung again, Marcus easily deflecting the blow.

"So I take it this is an admission to your crimes?"

"I admit nothing. I am merely going to silence a peddler of lies."

He swung again, Marcus ducking, striking a counterblow across Valentin's chest that knocked the wind out of him, causing him to stumble backward. He quickly recovered, and took a defensive position.

Marcus smiled, attempting to control his breathing so he wouldn't appear as exhausted as he was, having gone without food or drink for almost a day, and sleep even longer. He would have to end this quickly, for he was certain Valentin was well fed and rested. "So now I am a liar, despite the proof I presented?" He thrust toward Valentin's chest, his sword deflected. "I say *you* are the liar, sir. And I hesitate to call you 'sir,' now that we know you are a murderer. You are no longer worthy of such an honorable title."

Valentin growled, raising both hands over his head, surging forward as he dropped his sword hard and fast, intending to cleave Marcus in two.

Though only if he remained still.

Marcus dove to his right, rolling on his good shoulder and recovering his feet, swinging his blade as he did so, catching Valentin's side, lifting his chainmail up with the tip of his blade, revealing his bare torso. Marcus shoved forward, burying his blade deep inside his opponent. Valentin cried out as Marcus twisted the blade, surging to his full height and tipping Valentin off his feet and onto the floor, Marcus continuing forward and putting his full weight on the hilt.

The blade hit stone, signaling it had passed completely through his opponent. Valentin's eyes bulged, his mouth spurting blood as his hand slowly lost its grip on his sword. He stared up at Marcus as he withdrew his weapon, holding the sword out for Simon, who rushed forward and took it. Marcus dropped to his knees beside Valentin and placed a hand on his head, all of the Templars within the room bowing their heads as he recited the last rites.

A tear rolled down Valentin's cheek as he stared into Marcus' eyes, fear now ruling them, then he shuddered, his last gasps finally falling silent, as the prayer was completed.

Tears and sobs surrounded him as the ladies of the court were overwhelmed. Marcus rose and stepped away from the body, the pool of blood on the crisp white marble almost artistic in its contrast, shocking in its brutality. He bowed to King Philip, now standing, staring at the body of the commander of his Personal Guard.

And he finally spoke.

"The only crimes committed here today were that of Sir Valentin, and Sir Bernard. Sir Valentin has paid the ultimate price, and it is our decision that Sir Bernard should suffer the same fate. The rest of you we declare innocent of any crimes you have been accused of here today, and we wish you well."

With that, he departed through curtains behind the throne, his attendants following, his guard left rattled but still on watch. Marcus turned to the accused, still on their knees, and motioned for them to rise. "Come, my good men, my good *innocent* men! Rise, you are free!"

They looked at each other for a moment before smiles broke out and they rose, hugs and hearty handshakes exchanged, Marcus treated as the hero of the hour with promises of never-ending hospitality and more. He merely smiled, nodding, careful to accept none of the offers without disrespecting those making them.

After all, he was still a Templar, still avowed to a life of poverty, with a farm to work, and two young children to raise. Simon and David approached him, and hugs were exchanged, but no words. There was nothing to say, and frankly, he was all talked out. He couldn't remember the last time he had spoken so many words. In fact, he was certain that with the possible exception of reading memorized passages from the Bible aloud, he had probably never said so much at once, unrehearsed.

He actually felt some pride, and made a mental note to confess that sin the next time he saw the priest. As the Templar Knights filed out of the palace, Marcus and his men followed, young Thomas in tow, and they soon found themselves in the courtyard, the knights quickly mounting their horses, the newly arrived guard, still outside the gates, standing down after being informed of what had just happened by a senior surviving member of the King's Personal Guard.

Marcus spotted Bernard standing not twenty paces away, held against the wall, surrounded by four guards. He was red, sweaty, and pacing back and forth in a rage that threatened to consume him.

At the moment, he was everything he had never

been described as. If anyone were to see him for the first time now, none could describe him as cowardly, an embarrassment, or a laughingstock. If anything, they'd describe him as a caged animal, filled with hate and rage, ready to pounce on anything if given the chance.

Marcus frowned. The King's sentence was clear, and he had no doubt it would be carried out swiftly.

Simon yelled out, spinning toward a now running Thomas, a dagger gripped in his hand, the blade glistening in the afternoon sun. He raced toward Bernard, a roar filling the air, a roar of sorrow, a roar of rage, a roar of determination. Bernard spun toward him, his eyes bulging as the guards stepped aside, allowing Thomas to plunge his liberated dagger into the belly of a shocked Bernard.

Marcus' eyes widened as the young man lifted the blade high, ensuring it was a deathblow, before pulling it out then tossing it aside as Bernard gasped his last breaths. The guards suddenly turned on Thomas, and Marcus surged forward, Simon and a dozen Templars quickly following with swords drawn. Marcus grabbed Thomas by the tunic and hauled him into the center of the quickly formed circle, pointing at the dying Bernard.

"Let this be the last death here today! The King ordered him dead, and the son of one of his victims delivered the punishment. Would any man here deny him that right?"

Nobody said anything, though a few heads shook.

"Good. Then we shall leave, in peace, and someone will administer the last rites to this murderer. Leave it to God to decide if he should burn."

Marcus, still gripping Thomas' tunic, marched him toward a horse and put him on it, then mounted another brought for him by David. They rode through the gates in the midst of the two hundred knights, and Marcus turned to the young man.

"Are you all right?"

Thomas' eyes were wide, his chest was heaving, probably in shock at what he had just done.

"Son?"

Thomas' head jerked toward Marcus. "What?"

"Are you all right?"

He thought for a moment. "I think so."

"What will you do now?"

He shrugged. "I'm not sure. Try to keep my father's business going, I guess."

Marcus smiled. "I think he would be proud to hear you say that. Just the honest part though, right?"

Thomas chuckled. "I'm no talent like my father."

Marcus slapped him on the back. "I'm happy to hear that." He thought for a moment, then said something that surprised him. "If you ever find yourself desperate enough to think you may stray to the wrong side of what is right, seek me out. I'll be working my humble farm in Crécy-la-Chapelle. You're welcome to join us at any time."

Thomas nodded. "I-I just might do that." He smiled. "Thank you."

And before Marcus could say anything else, Thomas urged his horse forward, and he cut through the knights beside them, disappearing into the city streets he had grown up in.

Simon watched after him. "Do you think we'll ever

see him again?"

Marcus frowned. "I fear we will." He sighed. "But if we do, there's plenty of room on the farm."

Crécy-la-Chapelle, Kingdom of France

"You're back!"

Sir Marcus turned to see Bailiff's Delegate Archambault rush from his tiny office, his hat in hand. "Yes."

"And, umm, were you successful in your task?"

"Yes."

"Then who did it? Who committed the murders? Was it Templars like they say?"

Marcus halted his horse, staring down at the man as a crowd began to surround them. "Like *who* say?"

"Umm, well, the men who came to arrest Mr. Fabron. They said Templars were plotting against the King, and that they had murdered Mr. Fabron and his wife to cover up their crimes."

Marcus' blood boiled. "All lies. It turns out that some of the King's Personal Guard faked the evidence, murdered a Templar delegation from the Holy Land, and used their clothing to disguise themselves as Templars and commit the murders."

"Is this true?" asked someone in the crowd. "What proof do you have?"

"I'm here, aren't I? If the crimes we Templars had been accused of were true, then we would have been arrested. Instead, the King has heard the evidence, dismissed the charges, and those responsible have been brought to justice."

Archambault nearly crumpled his hat. "Justice?"

"They're in God's hands now."

Archambault made the sign of the cross. "And what will you do now? Will you return to the Holy Land?"

Marcus shook his head. "You know my plans. I intend to remain here and work the farm and raise my niece and nephew." He eyed him. "Why, do you have a problem with that?"

Archambault quickly backed away several steps, shaking his head. "No, umm, no, it's just that, well."

Marcus tensed. "What? What is it?"

"Umm, there's been a fire."

Marcus' chest tightened, and he urged his horse forward, the villagers gathered barely having enough time to get out of the way, as he charged through the small cluster of buildings and into the farmland lining either side of his path. As he came over a crest in the road, he gasped, slowing down as he saw the barn, completely razed by fire.

"Jacques! Angeline!" He raced toward the apparently unscathed farmhouse, no signs of life evident. Then he heard barking. "Tanya!"

The dog tore around the house, and he leaped from his horse, the dog jumping into his arms, licking his soiled face. Three little squeals of delight raced into sight, their arms outstretched, and he dropped to his knees, hugging them hard, thanking God that He had watched over them.

"Well, it's about time!"

He glanced up to see Isabelle standing in the doorway of the house, wiping her hands on an apron. "You said two days, and it's been more than that." She walked toward them, a hand out, ushering the children back. "You said you'd send word."

"It was difficult, what with being arrested for treason."

Her eyes bulged. "You were arrested?"

"Yes. I was to be put to death. So was David."

Simon leaned forward, jabbing a thumb at his chest. "*I* saved the day."

Marcus grinned. "That he did. With a little help."

David nodded. "This is true. You've never heard anyone speak so eloquently to the King. Sir Marcus saved a *lot* of lives."

"The bravest man I know. He even felled a mighty knight in the King's court."

"Sliced him open in front of everyone."

"Easily twice his size."

"You've never seen such a man."

Marcus shook his head, holding up a hand. "They exaggerate, I assure you."

But Isabelle wasn't hearing him, her cheeks flushed, her breathing rapid, her eyes fixated on him as if he were the only thing in the world. She appeared as if she might faint.

He glanced over at Simon and David, both with grins.

Then he stopped.

"Where's Jeremy?" He pointed at the barn. "And what happened here?"

Isabelle finally snapped out of whatever was happening to her and sighed, wiping her forehead with the back of her hand. "You wouldn't believe what has happened here." She jabbed a finger at the village. "They burned it!"

Marcus' jaw dropped. "What?"

"They burned it! They heard that you Templars were plotting against the King, that you had murdered Mr. Fabron, so they came here to burn everything. Luckily, Jeremy had just arrived, and he fought them off, but not before the barn was set afire. He managed to save the animals but was almost killed." She gestured toward Tanya, sitting on her haunches, panting up at Marcus, her tail wagging furiously. "That creature saved him. She went into the flames and pulled him out."

Marcus smiled at the dog and she began to rise, anticipating some attention. "Where is he?"

"Inside. I put him in your bed."

Marcus and the others went inside to find Jeremy propped up on several pillows, a cup of water in his hand.

David snorted. "You'll never get rid of the smell now."

Simon agreed. "Better to burn the place."

"Haha. Good to see you too."

Marcus walked over to his squire and sat on the edge of the bed. "I understand I owe you my thanks."

"I'll settle for not having to kiss your royal ass."

Marcus chuckled. "You're a good man." Tanya poked her nose into the proceedings, and Jeremy scratched her behind the ear.

"Thanks to this girl, I'm alive to enjoy the accolades."

David grunted. "I think he's faking it. I say we put him to work rebuilding the barn. After all, we all need some place to sleep."

Jeremy faked falling faint, his hands flopping out to his sides, his head rolling back. "Oh, I'm so weak…"

Simon swatted his feet. "Kiss his royal ass."

"Oh no! They're back!" cried Isabelle from the front of the house.

Marcus rushed out of the room, followed by the others, Tanya racing ahead and out the door, barking. He rushed past Isabelle and into the sunlight to see several dozen villagers coming up the path. He reached for his sword when Archambault waved at him with a smile, and he noticed that the men were carrying tools, and the women food and drink.

"Sir Marcus! Sir Marcus! So sorry to startle you!"

Marcus snapped his fingers at Tanya, and she stopped her snarling and returned to his side, sitting.

"We, umm, they, umm." Archambault shrugged. "*We* felt bad about the misunderstanding, so we've come to make amends. We want to rebuild your barn."

Shame was written on many of the faces, clearly belonging to those who had taken part in the crime. And while part of him would like to lay a good beating down on them, if he was going to live in this village and make it his home, he would need friends.

He stepped forward, smiling broadly. "Then we welcome you! All is forgiven and forgotten!"

Smiles spread, and the crowd pressed forward, the men heading to the barn, the women laying out blankets for what he was sure would prove to be a feast fit for kings.

"Umm, Sir Marcus, there is one matter we need to discuss."

Marcus turned to Archambault. "What?"

"Well, umm, I'm not sure how to say this, but word came back from Paris. Young Pierre, here, has no surviving family. He will have to go to an orphanage."

Pierre burst into tears, and Marcus spun toward the boy, not aware the poor child was within earshot. He dropped to a knee and reached out for the boy who rushed into his arms. "Please, sir, don't make me go!"

Marcus gave him a hug then pushed him back so he could look him in the eyes. "How would you feel about staying with us?"

Pierre beamed, his eyes widening. "C-can I?"

Marcus glanced over his shoulder at Archambault. "Well?"

Archambault shrugged. "I don't see why not."

Marcus turned back to Pierre. "Then it's settled. You'll stay with us, if you wish it."

Pierre bounced in place, barely containing his glee. "I do! I do!"

Marcus laughed, then swatted him on the bottom. "Now go play with the others, and stay out of the way. There's work to be done." He rose and stared at the villagers at work, Simon, Jeremy, and David at his side, Isabelle in the doorway.

Simon looked at him. "Do you think we can do this?"

Marcus surveyed the sight before his eyes, and goosebumps rushed over his body, an almost spiritual rapture erupting from within. And he smiled.

"With the good Lord on our side, how can we fail?"

THE END

ACKNOWLEDGMENTS

The idea for this novel came from a discussion with my father. I had known for some time that I wanted to write a novel about the Templars, that dealt exclusively with them. For those of you who read my James Acton Thrillers, you will probably have already enjoyed The Templar's Relic (four weeks on the USA Today list) and The Templar's Revenge. While those books have historical elements, they were still mostly focused on the modern day action.

I wanted something different.

The concept of the wounded warrior, forced to return home, was already there, and I had the idea that he would be forced to solve some crime. During the spit-balling session, I blurted out that he was some sort of Templar detective. I made note of the idea by sending myself an email with "TEMPLAR DETECTIVE" in the subject line, and continued the conversation.

But those two words continued to gnaw at me, and the next day I realized that they were the key, and The Templar Detective was born. I Googled it, in quotes, and found only three hits on the entire Internet, none of which had to do with anything related to what I was thinking about.

Three hits.

Almost unheard of these days.

This novel is dedicated to a man named Ken Arundel. He was my first real boss when I was a teenager, and challenged me to learn new things, despite my resistance. I was a computer geek, rare back then, and actually taught programming to gifted children, and basic computer skills at the local college. At sixteen, I was hired as a research assistant, and when he realized I actually could code, he wanted me to work on something in a language called CLIPPER (that sound you just heard were fellow veteran geeks the world over oohing in recognition). I wanted to work in WordPerfect macros, but he insisted.

So I reluctantly agreed.

And it led to a career in the IT world that would surprisingly prepare me for my eventual life as a full-time writer.

In the strange world of coincidences, about fifteen years later, the organization I worked for under Ken ordered a software product from the company I founded about five years after working for him. I immediately recognized the organization's name, and in an even greater coincidence, I recognized the last name of the woman who had placed the order.

I sent her an email, and it turned out she was indeed the sister of one of my best friends who had died tragically in a car accident when he was barely 18. Some might remember I once dedicated a book to my two friends, Garry and Daryl, who died so horribly.

It was a tearful exchange, so many memories dragged back to the surface for both of us, and that was when I learned Ken Arundel had recently died.

A man, who by pushing me to learn new things that were actually relevant in the business world, gave me my start.

And with this new series, quite different than

anything I've done before, I felt dedicating it to him was appropriate.

Thank you, Ken. You are missed.

With life in the Middle Ages being much simpler, there aren't a lot of people to thank this time. As usual, I'd like to thank my dad for the research, with a caveat that if there are any historical inaccuracies, they are mine alone. I'd also like to thank Deborah Wilson for some equine and canine help. Thanks as always to my wife, daughter, mother, and friends, for their continued support, and of course to the proofreading and launch teams!

To those who have not already done so, please visit my website at www.jrobertkennedy.com then sign up for the Insider's Club to be notified of new book releases. Your email address will never be shared or sold.

Thank you once again for reading.

Printed in the USA
CPSIA information can be obtained
at www.ICGtesting.com
CBHW011455280124
3771CB00043B/1018

9 780991 814220